THE VISIBILITY OF THINGS
LONG SUBMERGED

WINNER OF THE BOA SHORT FICTION PRIZE

THE VISIBILITY OF THINGS LONG SUBMERGED

Stories

George Looney

BOA EDITIONS, LTD. † ROCHESTER, NY † 2023

First Edition
23 24 25 26 7 6 5 4 3 2 1

For information about permission to reuse any material from this book, please contact The Permissions Company at www.permissionscompany.com or e-mail permdude@ gmail.com.

Publications by BOA Editions, Ltd.—a not-for-profit corporation under section 501 (c) (3) of the United States Internal Revenue Code—are made possible with funds from a variety of sources, including public funds from the Literature Program of the National Endowment for the Arts; the New York State Council on the Arts, a state agency; and the County of Monroe, NY. Private funding sources include the Max and Marian Farash Charitable Foundation; the Mary S. Mulligan Charitable Trust; the Rochester Area Community Foundation; the Ames-Amzalak Memorial Trust in memory of Henry Ames, Semon Amzalak, and Dan Amzalak; the LGBT Fund of Greater Rochester; and contributions from many individuals nationwide. See Colophon on page 152 for special individual acknowledgments.

Cover Design: Daphne Morrissey
Cover Art: "Alligator Swamp" by Aidong Ning
Interior Design and Composition: Isabella Madeira
BOA Logo: Mirko

BOA Editions books are available electronically through BookShare, an online distributor offering Large-Print, Braille, Multimedia Audio Book, and Dyslexic formats, as well as through e-readers that feature text to speech capabilities.

Cataloging-in-Publication Data is available from the Library of Congress.

State of the Arts

NYSCA

BOA Editions, Ltd.
250 North Goodman Street, Suite 306
Rochester, NY 14607
www.boaeditions.org
A. Poulin, Jr., Founder (1938-1996)

NATIONAL
ENDOWMENT
for the ARTS
arts.gov

ALSO BY GEORGE LOONEY

CONTENTS

Wish I could be a holy saint or a person without any feelins,
a poor idiota *like that Hector; or just a boy, a boy without the*
changing and hurtin that comes to you in a while, before you
know it you done changed from something skippin along or off
singin by yourself to a secret something lookin and huntin and
wantin in the dark, lets you know what you got on you and the
wild feelins that can come from what you got on you, wish I
could go to a magician and have him wipe them off of me with
a magic wand or with the wave of a silken handkerchief, or
in a puff of smoke; or just paint over them as you can do on a
picture.

—William Goyen, from *Arcadio*

WHAT GIVES US VOICE

Preacher

My voice brought them in, but the boy's hands healed them. They'd come and sit in stained clothes starched stiff and sweat and listen till their throats started in to constricting and they had to shout or swear in tongues. Sometimes they tore their clothes and asked to be flayed. Remember one time this woman threw herself on the altar and writhed and wrapped her shining legs round the cross and called out to Jesus. Said she was empty and rotted out. No matter how much water she drank, she said, nothing passed out of her, and her throat, it stayed dry. Said she knew all about guilt. That I believed. The way her legs held to the cross I was sure of it. Said she needed to be touched and healed. And the boy, he did touch her and heal her and left her cowering in the shreds of her clothes behind the altar, though he didn't seem to know nothing bout guilt, or the pain I seen him take from hundreds of men and women.

Wonder where all that pain went when he took it from them. Didn't seem to go into him. Never so much as seen him wince during a healing. Pain's got to go somewhere though. Like that Einstein fellow said bout matter and energy, can't neither be created nor destroyed. All it can do is change form. Healing is a mystery. But the boy, he had the gift. No question.

I've known other healers in my day. Worked with some of the best. Remember one, was named Jebediah, used snakes. They wasn't poisonous. Not at first. He used harmless garter snakes. Wherever the show stopped, an hour after we'd got the tent up we'd see Jebediah bent over and hunching along in a nearby field. Every now and then he'd disappear into the tall, seeded grass. There was always a strange humming in the air, too. It was Jebediah. That humming called the snakes out somehow, and every time he come back with a bag full of harmless snakes.

Later, he'd call the afflicted up to where he'd be standing with a snake in one hand and a cross in the other, get them down on their knees and confessing, and when he'd heard enough he'd stop them and ask Do you love God, Do you love Jesus? They'd be sobbing and would start chanting, Yes, I love Jesus, Yes, I love God, their broken or withered bodies swaying with whatever hymn Rachel was blasting out on the organ. Rachel was Jebediah's wife and one hell of an organist. She could make the simplest, most devout tune into a demon that could burn you out as easy as save you. Old Jebediah didn't know it, but she was like that in bed too.

So, Jebediah, innocent and ignorant to so much in this world, is standing over this man or woman sick with sin with his cross and the snake he's whipping back and forth. Then he tells them to grab the cross in his hand. When they do, that snake in his other fist starts this queer little dance and, God's honest truth, that snake changes color. Turns from a plain old green to red with black bands. And it grows right there in Jebediah's hand. Sometimes it grows so much in his hand, a big hand, beefy some might say, that snake almost bursts Jebediah's fingers apart and escapes. But in the three summers Jebediah travelled with us, never once saw a snake get away from him. Can't say the same bout Rachel. She was always getting off to somewhere with some sinner or the other. And she could change color, too.

These red bands would come out round her breasts and up her neck to her chin.

According to Jebediah, the sin and the pain from them broken bodies went into the snakes and become poison. Jebediah said he had to be careful after the healing. One bite, he'd say, and it'd be over. They was poisonous after taking in all that suffering, he said, and he'd have to break their necks soon as they changed color. When he did, Rachel's practiced hands would be in the air and her foot would be hard on the pedal that cuts off sound, and everyone in the tent would hear the echo of that snap of a neck and fall to their knees and praise God. It was truly a miracle to watch. But thing is, maybe a snake's body ain't big enough to hold all that sin. Maybe some got into Rachel's organ playing, and Rachel herself. Maybe what we see with our eyes is less than we ever thought it was. Sure would explain some things, if that was so.

Don't know whatever happened to Jebediah. One summer he didn't join us, and that was that. Couple years later thought I saw Rachel in a congregation outside a small town somewhere in Georgia. But she didn't come up for the boy to touch her. Might not have been her. Though that night, I remember, I was having a hell of a time getting to sleep and just as I was bout to drop off, as they say, I heard a humming somewhere outside, and thought it was Rachel, that she was calling the snakes up for Jebediah. Or maybe herself. The next morning, I passed right by a man cooking up a snake red with black bands. Mystery is the state we live in, everywhere.

But with Jebediah there was at least something you could see, something that said, This is where the sin goes; this is what holds the pain. With the boy, least at first, there was nothing to see. That worried me. Most of the healers I've worked with were troubled, so I got close to them, kind of a father confessor thing. That's how I knew old Jebediah had no clue when it come to Rachel. He'd spend hours drinking in some foul motel room, weeping and saying how much he loved that woman. To hear him tell it, her flesh was so white, and he meant pure, untouched even, that he couldn't look at her cept out of the corners of his eyes. He'd say how she looked, this wavering form of light and goodness, and I couldn't see any woman I'd ever known. First time he confessed, said they'd been together two years and he'd not touched her once. Said he didn't deserve her. Said that a lot, then he'd weep some whiskey right out his nose.

But the boy never come to me and confessed nothing. Funny, ain't it, how you don't think you know a body till you know the wrong they've done, and the pain they carry on their backs cause of it. With the boy, there didn't seem to be nothing weighing him down. A strong gust and he'd have been lost. Don't know, maybe he was just a creature too light for this earth. Like I said, I've worked with lots of healers, and the boy's the only one ever scared me. And with them damn gators, it got worse. Couldn't hardly sleep at all without dreaming bout one of them pulling me down into water dark and cold as the devil hisself. And the boy just watching from above, up there where, somewhere not far off, a hymn's being played on a windy organ by a woman mad with love.

Sister

Remember when he was ten, before the visions, before the lines of people in pain started forming round the house, my little brother, he come out one morning into the back yard and stood over this dry well wearing just the bottoms of his Green Hornet PJs. I watched him from that upstairs window, right there, that the sun was glazing into a swamp of light. Must of been painful to look at from out there, but he wasn't looking at it. Wasn't exactly looking at anything. Eyes was closed as a matter of fact. Remember wondering how he'd made it out there through the kitchen and the parlor, both of which was always cluttered mornings with his toys, without his eyes open. Don't know why I guessed his eyes had been closed the whole time, but turned out they had been, that he was what they call sleepwalking. Maybe I didn't guess his eyes had been closed at the time. May be I only remember it that way.

But there he was, his scrawny chest and arms almost glowing in the morning light, standing over the well. His eyes was closed, like I said, remember that much for sure, but if they'd been open he'd of been gazing right down into that well. Though the cement slab was over the actual opening, so even if his eyes had been open he wouldn't really of been looking into the well, but at a plain cement slab. But I remember thinking, despite his closed eyes and the definite fact of the slab, that that's what he was doing, gazing into the well. Ain't that strange?

Remember it was a Saturday morning. I could just hear the TV playing downstairs. Cartoons. Remember I heard a thunk. Must of been the coyote falling after running off one of them towers of rock I know really exist some places out in the southwest. I've seen them, and can't seem to laugh at the coyote anymore. Ain't that strange? When I heard the thunk, I pictured the puff of smoke that always blossomed, like some desert flower, and wondered if he'd been watching TV with his eyes closed, and what he'd seen if he had.

He just stood there, eyes closed, glowing in the sunlight. What happened next can't never forget. A cat, a stray tiger stripe he'd often tried to tame, that he'd leave food out for and talk to softly from a distance, just walked over to him there, calm as you please, and started rubbing gainst his legs. Might of even been purring. His eyes still closed, my little brother bent down and with his puny arms moved that cement slab so it was just off the opening to the well. I'd never of guessed he could move something so solid. Ain't it strange the way we think of strength most of the time? Almost called to my mother then, figuring it'd be best if she got out there and pulled him away from the well, but what happened next kept me at that window with my trap shut, as they say. Soon as he'd finished moving the slab and stood up to keep gazing down in the well he could actually see now, or could of seen if his eyes had been open, which they wasn't, that stray just walked over the opening and fell in, just like the coyote in the cartoon that was still playing downstairs on the TV. Ain't the world strange?

Believer

Tain't no mystery to it. The boy was just touched by God. First time saw him take that gator down, I just knew I was in the presence of The Holy Trinity. Who else could take down a beast like that? A boy on his own? No way. Remember thinking someone should get a picture of him top that broken gator. With that spotlight coming from behind him, was a kind of acension. That first time, everone stepped back when the boy had some workers open the box on the platform a preacher'd done a little preaching on afore bringing the boy up to do some healing. Needs what's in there, I thought. Something in the box lets him heal, I figured, but never thought it'd be a gator, and a big one at that. Must of been twenty-five feet from its ugly grin to its tail. I stepped back with everone else, and some of the women and children screamed. Fear can hit us over and over, like a bruised woman who's had enough and keeps swinging the skillet past the point where the husband's protesting or moving at all. Don't stick around long, though. Fear likes to get in and out afore it's recognized. Recognition, like the good Lord says, is poison to fear. Says so in the Bible, somewhere.

So the boy asks everone to come close. Tells us not to fear nothing, as we is in the company of the Lord, and no beast can ignore that. Tells everone to sing a hymn, and the organist starts in playing "Come Thou Almighty" and everone standing round that platform where the gator's looking a bit confused, or so it seemed to me, we all start in singing. When we're singing *Spirit of holiness, on us descend*, the boy kneels right in front of that gator and puts his hands in the shape of prayer and that gator opens his mouth almost like a yawn, but don't move toward the boy a bit. The boy stays kneeling there the whole hymn. When the organist breaks into "A Mighty Fortress is Our God," the boy raises hisself tall as he can. Tain't much. The boy weren't even five foot, or, if he was, he was just that. Don't know bout no one else, but, God forgive me, that first time my faith weren't strong enough. Was sure that boy was going in that gator and not coming back. When we get to *Did we in our own strength confide, Our striving would be losing*, the boy lifts out his arms like he's on the cross and lowers his head. Don't know if he was praying or what, but his lips was forming some kinda words. His arms still out like he's hanging on the Lord's wood, the boy walks round that gator and gets its tail in his puny boy's arms and twists it in a way you know ain't natural. The gator seems to shiver its whole body, but don't make a sound. The boy climbs right up on its back and puts his arms round the gator's neck. Almost like he's hugging the gator. Almost looks like love, and for a breath I'm not sure what's happening. Then, just as we get to *For still our ancient foe Doth seek to work us woe*, the boy pulls hisself up and the gator's head with him, in a way that sure ain't natural, and the gator's smile closes and it's done. The organist starts up with "Nearer My God to Thee," and the boy slides down off the gator and kneels aside it, one of his small hands stroking its back like it were a pet he'd just put down. When we sing *Angels to beckon me, Nearer, my God, to Thee*, the boy raises up the gator's head and makes the cross over it, almost as if to say that gator was an angel. Ain't love a mystery? Can't put my finger on it now, but I knew then something miraculous had happened, and it had to do with love. God is love, we're told, and it's love that subdues the beast. Was married thirty-three years, and I believe it.

After that first time, remember how there was people who said the gator'd been drugged, that the boy was never at risk, said it was all a show. So many people find faith hard to believe in. But I was there that first time, and three others, too, and close enough to see the lust in the gator's eye, and I don't doubt it was love made it lie there and let itself be broken for our sins. And no one can doubt the power it give the boy. After he busted that gator, he healed hundreds. I witnessed them healings myself, and can attest to them. The boy healed just bout everone who let God's love in their bodies, and made each man and woman and child take a hunk of that gator home for dinner. It was damn good eating.

Preacher

Wonder sometimes, Did someone heal Jebediah? Is that why he never come back to us? A woman, the good Lord says, can break you. One even broke Him, back in the garden. Wonder what color that snake was, if it was full of poison and red banded black. Like to think so. Something should make sense in this world.

Did someone heal Jebediah of Rachel? Old Jebediah, who lay beside her at night without touching her, wasn't alone in needing to be healed of her. Some nights I thought of going to the boy in his room in whatever motel we was staying in and asking him to hear my confession. Maybe I should have told him bout Rachel, bout those nights she'd lay me down and sit atop me and I'd be inside her and moving with her and she'd be moaning and then in the midst of everything she'd wrap one of them red, black-banded snakes Jebediah had broke the necks of round my neck and start to tighten it. Got so tight I couldn't breathe as she bucked and moaned and cursed till she collapsed atop me, the weight of her thin and shivering body a kind of guilt. Haven't touched Rachel in years, but the guilt still lays atop me some nights, sets me to shivering.

That summer I thought I'd seen her in Georgia I shut things down and spent weeks looking for her. Must have looked crazy, a preacher looking so desperate for an organist, no matter how good she was with the music. We can lose our way so easy, the good Lord tells us.

While I was searching for the woman whose sin had left me as poisonous as Jebediah's snakes, with a burning no hand nor body could put out but her, I found Zachary. Zachary was on the road like me, searching after a brother no one had seen or heard from in years. So many souls searching in faith and without faith for someone. That's what this world is, the crossroads of all that searching.

Zachary was a believer. Nights he'd spend hours on his knees in fields or in rancid motel rooms, when either of us had the money, praying to God he might find his brother and bring him home. After he'd prayed hisself out we'd sit and talk. I learned how his brother had killed a girl by mistake and left town crying and calling the girl's name, almost like he believed she was only hiding somewhere. Dear Jesus, is all of us gone searching? Zachary said his brother'd been in love with the girl, that they'd been sinning and one night without knowing it he'd squeezed her neck till she couldn't breathe and died. Good Lord, I thought, when Zachary told me his brother's sad story, is that what I'm looking for out here chasing after

Rachel and leaving my service to God behind? Was I looking to die breathless in Rachel?

It was while I was gone searching the boy found his first gator and learned what he could do. If I hadn't been off searching, he might never have gone to the swamp. And if it hadn't been for my searching for sin I'd not have seen Zachary's brother in that revival, and might have come down hard on the boy when I come back and refused his wrestling with the gators. But we did find Zachary's brother in the revival. Course, I'd been hoping to find Rachel in the crowd. I was still burning then, though that's so long over now it's hard to remember clearly, sitting there in that tent with the stench of farmers and their wives sweating in the damp heat and my own heat rising and itching and the ground so damp from weeks of rain it was almost swamp. And the mosquitoes settling on all of us like they was after the sin that'd brought each of us to that tent.

Remember how Zachary stiffened beside me when the healer was brought up. When he heard his brother's name, Phineas, in the mouth of the preacher, he started shaking and crying, but he didn't cry out and run to him. Instead, after his brother's first healing was done, he turned to me and smiled, said Jesus had taken care of everything, after all. Then he got up and left the tent. Heard he was found beside a road hanging from an oak, breathless. Who can understand this world?

As for Phineas, the murderer brother, his healing was miraculous. He'd have the afflicted kneel before him and quote The Lord's Prayer. Then he'd bring a worm out of a bucket sitting beside him. But these weren't no ordinary worms. Never seen nothin like them. Heard they live in swamps in Louisiana and ain't found nowhere else. Don't know if that's true, but I know I've never seen them cept in Phineas' hands. He'd tell the man or woman or child to hold the worm, to whisper to it the tale of their affliction. Then he'd take it back and, I swear this is true, he'd swallow that worm head to tail intact. It would crawl down his throat and into his organs science tells us are miles long. Phineas would stand there and a spotlight would show the worm wriggling through his body so we knew it was really there. We could see it moving down his chest, past his heart, which it must have wanted to eat but didn't, into his stomach. Lower than that we could only guess at the worm's movements. In just a minute though, we'd see that worm coming back up, like it'd pulled a U-turn in Phineas' body. It left the heart alone again and come right back out his mouth. This was Phineas' way of swallowing the sin and suffering for others without being poisoned. When the worm come back out the sinner was healed, and Phineas told the man or woman or child to take the worm home and cut it in pieces and bury each piece in their yard saying the prayer for the burial of the dead over every planting.

Tried to get him to come back with me, but he told me Jesus had set his path and I couldn't argue. Did learn, though, the girl Phineas had killed by mistake had been promised to Zachary in the way some families still do, and Zachary'd sworn to find Phineas and kill him for what he done. Told him that Zachary'd been with me and seen him swallow the worm and smiled and left. Couldn't tell him bout the hanging from the oak. Heard that later and, besides, might not be true. You can only believe what you see in this world. Everything else is belief in another world, or nothing.

Sister

Everyone was in love with my brother, or scared of him, or both. Even the preacher didn't know how to take him. Even before the wrestling with gators. Ain't it strange? Was just after preacher shut down the tour. A temporary measure, remember him saying. Remember him saying the Lord had called him and him alone on a quest, that's the word he used. A different revival come to the outskirts of town, and the story was this revival had a healer who swallowed worms. My brother went one night and took me with him. He left before the service was done. It was those worms that put it in his mind he needed something, and sent him off to the local swamp to find it.

I stayed the whole service, and more. God forgive me, never saw a man holier than Phineas. God he was a huge man, and gentle. His tongue was a worm inside me and I cried out to Jesus more than I ever had. After, we prayed together and he told me the story of how he come on the worms, or they come on him. Depends on which way you look at it, don't it? Guess that's true of most things. Ain't that strange?

Phineas told me how he'd been a sinner for so long thought the Lord must sure of given up on him. Phineas talked bout women and drink and violence. Phineas was the kind of man who could as easily snap a neck as turn it red with passion. Phineas told me a husband had caught him in bed with his wife and had shot him in the back with him still moving over the woman. Said he'd come to in the swamp, a dark place and filled with demons. Said he lay in that bitter water for days before he could move at all. Said he'd of died if not for the healing powers of that decaying mud oozing into his wound. Said he had just enough strength to hold his head out of the water. Said it was Jesus that sent the worms to feed him. Said Jesus told him to let the worms in and they'd nourish him, but not to bite down, to let the worm do the work. The first time was rough. Phineas said took all his faith in Jesus to let the worm swim into him. Said the worm crawling through him hurt like nothing he'd ever felt. Said he almost sunk under the stinking water and drowned hisself. But once the worm come back out his mouth and swam off, Phineas said he felt stronger and full. The passing of the worm through his body had fed him in some way he needed to be fed. Ain't it strange how sometimes it ain't food we need to go on?

Phineas said Jesus told him to take some worms from the swamp and heal others. Said since them days in the swamp, he'd followed the Lord's path and stayed clear of his old sinning ways. Until me, he said. Said the Lord had sent me to him to heal him in ways the worms couldn't. And it was while I was healing the worm swallower my brother went off to the swamp looking for the Lord. Ain't it strange, the places we look for Jesus? Even stranger, the places we find him. Felt Him there every time with Phineas. At times seemed it was Jesus atop me, and I'd stretch out my arms in the shape of the cross right there on the damp sheets. Our love was truly a holy love.

My brother never did talk much, but the night he come back dragging the gator behind him he told a story. Don't know if it's true. Only God and my brother and the gator know the truth. Said he'd lain down in the putrid water of the swamp, with all that dying and decaying surrounding him like a kind of music. Was a hymn, he said, the most beautiful he'd ever heard. My brother said he lay in that filth for three nights. On the third night, he said, he saw a light moving between the sagging trunks of the trees. Said he followed that light and it led him to the den of sleeping gators. Said he lay down right there with all them gators and slept the first time in three nights. Said he thought of Jesus crossing the desert in the midst of all them lepers and sinners with other afflictions. Said that's how he felt laying down with the gators. The sleep of gators, he said, is a holy thing. Nothing like it in the world, he said.

Said in the morning it come to him what he needed to do. Said it must of been Jesus speaking to him through the living sounds of the swamp. Said a gator woke and swum right up to him and raised its long head right into his arms like an offering. When he broke its neck, he said, the light that led him to the gators appeared over the water and he watched it rise into the light of the sky and disappear. Said he felt his heart shake itself in his chest, like it was shrugging off a long sleep. Guess consecrated killing, think that's what he called it, forgave what he done with strays round the house when he was younger. That dry well had so many bodies rotting in it, by the time the preacher come and enlist my brother in the Lord's work, that it stunk for blocks. No one could figure where the stench was coming from. I knew, but didn't tell no one. Was too scared from watching him morning after morning sleepwalking and killing them dazed animals. Ain't it strange sometimes how the Lord chooses to call us? Used the murdering of gators to heal a boy and through the boy, others. Used my flesh to heal a man passed through by worms in a swamp. Ain't it strange?

Believer

Martha was the only one the boy couldn't heal. We brought that hunk of gator home after the boy had touched her and told her to fry it up and serve it with baked taters and carrots simmered in its juices. Did just what the boy said. Was good eating. Martha and me both dug in and ate like we hadn't in' years. We couldn't get enough, it seemed. The gator was tender and smelled like a slice of heaven. We was sure she was healed, so sure we did something we hadn't done in years. That night, after gorging ourselves on the gator and fixins, we lay atop the sheets, both of us naked the way the good Lord made us. I rolled over and held her frail body in my arms. She was shivering and Jesus did she feel good there, her naked flesh warming up gainst mine. Got on top of her and she pushed gainst me at first, force of habit I guess. She was moaning, though, and saying words I couldn't make out, and I put myself hard inside her and I could feel her shiver almost as though she was crying and God it felt good I could move her like that. Could smell that gator as I moved over her. Both of us were breathing that gator alive into the room with us, and it was a blessing, I thought.

Next morning, Martha was gone aside me. Gone and cold in our bed. The preacher come and give her body the rites, and the boy come too and cried a little over my Martha, consecrating her with his tears. One failure didn't shake my faith, though, even if it was my Martha. The boy was the real thing, no doubt.

The boy healed me bout a month after Martha died. I'd been sleeping out in the shed. Couldn't lie down in the bed where I'd slept right through her passing. Cursed myself all the time, so much no one would talk to me. Everone thought I was crazed with grief, and they was right. Got so I couldn't stand seeing couples out walking, it put me in a rage and I took to breaking things. First, in my own home. But got so bad at times I broke whatever was around, no matter where I was at the time. Neighbors shut their doors to me. I was cast out, just like Satan. Can't say as I blame them. I broke things cause I was broken. Wanted the world to be like me. Wanted to feel right again in the world. I was selfish.

It was the boy who called me to kneel afore him and bless the Lord, and his hands over my heart that calmed me and told me to lie once more in the bed Martha and I had shared. With me kneeling there afore him, he spoke in my Martha's own sweet voice. Said everthing was all right. Said let that old demon guilt go. Said she was with God now and beyond ever poison of the flesh. Said go on and fix all them things you broke, and keep fixing things long as you can. It was Martha saying this. I know her voice. And it was so sweet and calm and wise I put my arms round the boy and cried and cried and he pronounced me healed.

Since then I been fixing things like Martha told me. Everone lets me in now, and I do the Lord's work by keeping things people cherish in this life going. But if not for the boy, Lord knows what I'd of broken, afore I finally broke myself.

Preacher

Believing don't come easy to most. Most wrestle with the world as it seems and try to make that speak for the spirit. But when it comes to the soul, the world's mute. Probably deaf, too. Like Jebediah was made deaf by his passion. Never heard Rachel. Never heard her moaning. Never heard her cry out or the shivering of her body, which I swear to the Lord Jesus had a sound all its own. Could've been the sound angels make, their wings grazing the world in passing. Was the most spiritual sound I ever heard, though that don't make what I done with another man's wife holy. Sin is what has weight to it. Sin is what keeps us in the world, can't deny it. Jebediah was a conduit for the sins of others, shuffling them off into snakes, but what he needed was some sinning of his own. Was what Rachel needed too, and from him.

Even the boy, turns out, knew of sinning. Least ways, his sister must have thought so. Something made her scared of him. Don't know what it was, but must stink all the way to heaven. Probably what broke them gators. Couldn't have been the boy alone. When he stroked the gator and whispered to it, most say he was praying with it, bringing it to God for a last redemption. Maybe he was telling it things even a gator couldn't stomach, stories of sins there's no prayer for, sins that stick in the throat of a gator so it suffocates. Sure makes sense what killed the gators weren't the boy, but sin. Course, this is the world and sense ain't common in it, no matter what folks say.

May be what brought them in wasn't my voice after all. May be it was sin brought them in. May be sin was what give me voice, what gives any of us voice.

Can't seem to get Rachel moving over me like a demon out of my mind. Burned, as they say, into my remembering. And them snakes killed in her husband's hand round my neck, sure that's a sign of the devil and the Lord wrestling over our loving in them ruined motel rooms at the edges of towns. There's a battle going on inside us, that's sure. It may be that battle's going on in the world itself, and we're just one bit of it. It may be we're nothing but bit players. May be the world's a scam played on us to take us for all we are. May be it's all a shell game, and the truth's been palmed. But it may be believing's our trump card. Like to think so. Like to think I'm holding something the world don't know bout, something I can drop on it just when I need to be weighed down. Believing is all bout not knowing, after all, and it's the not knowing we have to break or change to something else, something we can hold in our hands and see and show to everyone like Jesus showed Thomas his wounds.

It may be healing comes out of not knowing. Could be that's why the boy was the best healer I ever saw. Them gators he wrestled, he didn't need them. They was all show. Though got to admit they made a hell of a show. Better than snakes or swallowing worms or speaking in tongues or reciting dreams or prophesizing or any of the tricks I've come to recognize over the years as the trappings of faith. But truth is, none of them touches faith. Can't believe them gators did neither, but they was good eating. And no one ever griped bout the killing of gators to do the Lord's work here on earth.

Remember when I come back after giving up on finding Rachel, had dreams for weeks of desert landscapes and a mad music being played on some invisible organ. In some, Rachel was hanging from an oak, naked and pale and moving in a hot wind, her stiff body making a music that could swallow everything as is but not have a prayer of ever changing it. Once, I got naked and crawled up the tree and down the rope to her body and held on and hummed in her ear and every snake in the world come out of the ground to sway with my humming. Oh Lord, don't know what it is. This world is a mystery, and meaning's just another kind of faith we cling to down here like I clung to Rachel swinging from that tree. May be none of it matters, but remembering her body makes me need to know something for certain bout the world. Remembering how she hummed cross my flesh those nights in those sad motel rooms makes me feel I should have been looking for Jebediah stead of Rachel. Should have been looking to confess, to come clean as they say. Should have let go of Rachel's cold body and fallen to the snakes. Could be they'd have bitten me over and over and taken all the poison out. Should have given myself over to that swamp of swaying snakes. That would have been faith. Maybe I wouldn't have woke from the dream to see the inside of that gator. Wish I'd never heard of gators. Wish the boy had picked any other creature than that gator. Wish the boy had had the power of raising up, but only Jesus hisself could do that. Damn the swallowing and breaking this world is.

Lord forgive me, but it's just too much now and then. The good Lord works in mysterious ways, and all the proof I'll ever need was in the belly of that gator. In its belly and how I wallowed in its insides spilled cross that stage trying to hold her. How the stink of the gator's in my blood now. How my heart's gone scaly and full of hunger. How I wear round my neck a string with two bones clenched together at my heart, one bone a gator tooth, the other her finger. Like to think it's the one a ring slipped off of long ago, that love stripped to the bone is still more than hunger. God, they say, is love, after all. Don't want to think God is just hunger.

Sister

Was there the night that woman's hand and arm spilled out the gator's mouth when my brother broke its neck. First thought I had was of Jonah from the Old Testament in that whale and all. Guess in a whale there's room to live. That gator didn't have room for the woman. Been told she was an organist. Been told she could play hymns so they would burn out your heart. Guess that's why the preacher fell on what was left of her naked body and rolled with it in the slime of that gator's innards after that old man come up and gutted it open right there on stage. Never saw a stranger sight than that preacher clinging to what was mostly just a chest and head, though there might of been one leg hanging to it, clinging and rolling and calling Rachel over and over. Took five men to pull the preacher off what was left of the woman and carry him off the stage, him crying and saying Rachel and cursing God the whole time they was dragging him away.

My brother, he didn't heal no one that night. Sent everyone away. He come to me that night saying he needed to unburden hisself, that's how he put it. Told me bout the visions he'd had years before he started in to healing. They was nightmares of pain and suffering and cruelty. Some I could see connecting to what I'd seen round that well, that stinking cursed well, but others come from a place or places I never knew nothing bout. Places I still don't want to know nothing bout. Some things, he said, he'd never unburden hisself of. After telling me them visions, he put his arms round me and buried his head in my chest and cried and shivered. Never seen him that way before that night, and it was good. For once, we was like brother and sister, and after a bit he fell to sleep there in my arms and I stayed on holding him and kept watch for any demon that might be thinking bout putting one of them visions in his thoughts. That night I could of broken the neck of any demon, or anything living, to protect him. Seems we all need protecting of some sort or nother. Ain't that strange? Hard to tell who's the strongest when we is all so weak and easy to break.

Something broke in my brother that night there with the woman's hand and arm waving to him out of the mouth of that gator. Was a curse and a blessing, that breaking. Was a blessing cause it's what sent him to me to confess and find solace in the arms of his sister. Was a curse cause it took from him whatever calmed the gators to give up their bodies for the Lord's work.

Was the very next night it happened. My brother found a new preacher and spread the word, promising to heal those turned away the night before. Some did come, though not enough to fill the tent. Everything was fine till he told the men to let the gator out. God bless them, they hesitated. But my brother, he told them to do it, told them it'd be fine, and they believed him. Ain't it strange what we can believe? You could see their bodies trembling as they opened the box. Soon as it was open enough for the gator to get out, they jumped off stage. Never seen them do that before. Guess even the strongest faith only goes so far. Wish it wouldn't of gone far as it did. Wish they'd never opened that box.

Soon as they was off the stage, the tent got quiet and my brother got down on his knees and was praying The Lord's Prayer loud enough we could all hear it. Some of us started praying it along with him in shaky voices. Remember hearing that grainy sound of the gator moving bout in the box. Don't remember it ever being as loud as it was that night. The gator come out and turned to us and opened its mouth. That stopped our praying and some of us moved back a bit, just to be sure. My brother was the only one still praying and that gator turned and moved quicker than any gator I'd ever seen, though truth is the only gators I'd seen before that night was the sleepwalking gators my brother broke the necks of. That gator went right up to my brother and cut him in two with one bite. I swear to God my brother, separated from his knees, kept right on praying as the gator swallowed him, broken cept for his faith. That gator left my brother's knees still planted on the stage and headed for the back of the tent, in the direction of the swamp. Didn't try to bite anyone or anything else. Seemed calm, somehow. Seemed healed. Ain't that strange? I remember crying and holding my brother's legs in my arms. It come to me later one of my brother's visions had prophesied this. Strange, what we hear and what we don't, what we see and what we choose to believe.

Believer

It was me opened that gator so everthing spilled cross the stage. Saw it was the organist, Rachel, same as the preacher saw, and naked. Still can't forget the look on her face lying there surrounded by the foul carcass of the gator. Was almost angelic, like that gator had somehow healed her by swallowing her. Remember thinking that minus her arms she was like the goddess of love them Romans called Venus. Remember she was painted coming out of a shell over the water, like normal love tween a man and a woman weren't enough to birth a goddess. The Bible says somewhere God is love. Says God so loved the world, too. May be God so loved Rachel as to let her burning go out by being swallowed by a gator. Could see that.

Though wish I hadn't seen the preacher rolling in the blood and guts of that gator with what was left of her body. His face weren't angelic at all, but the face of some demon in that moment of grief. Dear Lord, the things that spewed out that preacher's mouth. Took all of us to drag him away from the half-eaten organist.

That was the oddest thing. Her body was either gone or ruined, eaten away at like the poisons we fill the air with these days eat at ever building in town. Sad ain't it, what we do to the world, what we're doing? But her face weren't touched. Like I said, was angelic.

I'll not be able ever to forget that preacher kissing that miraculous face. If that weren't love enough to birth a goddess, there's no hope in the world. Surrounded by all that slime and blood and stink, saw the preacher stop his rolling and thrashing and take her face in his hands so tender was almost not a touch and kiss her lips. Told that face he loved her. Said he always had. Told her he'd looked for her and that his looking had led to this, to him finding her in the belly of the beast. Started calling to Jebediah, begging forgiveness. Said some other things, too, made no sense, then he was rolling and thrashing and moaning again.

Never saw the preacher after we left him in a motel room that night, still weeping for Rachel, still asking Jebediah to forgive him. But seems to me someone should paint that preacher kissing that chewed up woman with the perfect face and use it for an icon. Should build a following round it, a religion whose doctrine is the hunger in the human heart to love, despite everthing. If God is love, surely that kiss was a burning illumination in this world of swallowing and darkness and breaking and suffering. No mystery to it. Just love, is all.

THE MUSIC OF A THING

"Her heart's all cud," Leroy shouts.

Riding shotgun, Jackson makes a noise that could be a chortle or a choking sound and sucks back the warm dregs of the last Stroh's. Dust off the back road we're barreling down swallows up the bottle Jackson hurls out his window. If it shatters not one of us hears it over the engine that's only hanging on due to Leroy's uncanny mechanical prowess. Jackson waited till the beer was all but gone and we were on our way back to town to bring up this business of him and Sarah.

All I can do is imagine her heart, any heart, stained green and being gently chewed on by the flat teeth of some nonchalant cow.

Around town Leroy's in demand. Lots of folks have cars that seem in almost constant need of Leroy's laying on of grimy hands. Men and women drive or drag their clunkers over to Leroy's and the women, they sit in the waiting room, or what passes for a waiting room—a couple of old wooden chairs Leroy stole out of the high school after the fire but before the wrecking ball—the women sit in those stiff chairs and watch Leroy touching their cars and they sweat and murmur things—I've heard them—filthy things, under their smoke-heavy breath. Jackson's told Leroy more than once, "They imagine you is touching *them*, not their cars."

Whenever Jackson tells him this Leroy just smiles and nods his head in sync with his "Sure, sure, Jackson." I don't say much when Leroy and Jackson are getting into it. Mostly I just listen. I've heard folks round here say it's a good thing Leroy don't have a clue when it comes to the fairer sex. Truth is, they say, if he did none of their cars would be running.

"What do you mean, Leroy, her heart's all cud? Cud like a cow's cud?"

"Listen," Leroy says. "All I'm saying is, she's fallen in and out of love enough she could write the holy scriptures of being fickle."

And that's true enough. Sarah started young, caught in the janitor's closet with that kid with the humped back when she was just thirteen. Rumor is, when Miss Perkins opened the door and flicked on the light Sarah had her ass on the edge of the utility sink and her thin gymnast's legs around his waist and, her head straining over his shoulder, she was trying to get as much of his hump in her mouth as she could. That must have been one hell of a hump, was the joke around school for weeks. Though what always struck me most was the idea of her lips trying to stretch wide enough to get that whole hump into her mouth. Like it was the deformity she was loving and not the boy.

Wonder whatever happened to him. As best I can recall, he left school right after that. Hell, can't even remember his name. Round here, he's just the nameless kid with a hump Sarah started with. Sometimes at night I try to imagine being that kid. Being, all my life, haunted by those furtive, fumbling moments in the dark in a tiny room surrounded by push brooms and filthy mops with a girl trying to suck every bit of my hump into her mouth while she pulled me all the way into her.

Was there enough light for him to see her reflection in the crud-covered mirror over the sink and to watch those almost childish lips stretch across the almost angular curve jutting from above his left shoulder blade? Is that something he got over, or does he size up every woman he meets by thinking about her mouth widened over his hump, what that would do to her lips?

"Doesn't matter how many times she's loved before," Jackson yells to Leroy. "Love ain't about timelines and the calculating of numbers," he says. And though Leroy's sarcastic "Yeah, right" makes it clear he isn't having any of what Jackson's saying, Jackson has it right. Love's not about who got where first. Nor is it a matter of adding up numbers as if it were some kind of equation, nor some sort of line-up where it's all about identifying who did what and who didn't. None of us is exactly innocent. And come to think of it, a heart that's all cud might just have it over one that's never been gnawed on at all.

All them women who've longed for Leroy's hands on their bodies, despite them being married or engaged or in grieving, I wonder what condition their hearts are in. If what gnaws at them while they squirm and sweat in the butt-polished pine of those chairs and watch Leroy bent over into the open maws of their cars is enough to make anything better for them?

"Some folks," Leroy said once, his hands so dark with grease that, with the lights out, you'd think someone had chopped them off and fed them to some hungry dogs, "they got the magic of music in their hands. Knew a kid once," he said, "Jason was what they called him. He could pick up a guitar or sit down at a keyboard and listen to a song once and play it perfect, note for note. Said he'd never had a lesson, too. Just had the love of making tunes," Leroy said. "It's the music of engines that gets me going," he said. "And when a note's being struck that's out of sync, or when a chord just ain't right, my hands, they can find where the machine's gone wrong and fix it."

"Someone told me," Leroy said, "that nowadays they got computers and all kinds of electronics they plug an engine up to and diagnose what's gone wrong. Guess that's some sort of progress, seeing that most folks can't hear the music engines make. Can't tell by the music where the problem is. The music of a thing is the best way, though," Leroy said, "to know what's what."

"What about the midget?" Leroy yells to Jackson over the engine. "I mean," he yells, "a woman who'll jump a midget and darn near rape him has got to give you pause, don't you think?"

The midget thing's another famous Sarah story. A midget Jehovah's Witness, the story goes, rang the doorbell when Sarah's mother was off visiting, and Sarah let him in as if she wanted to be saved when all she wanted was to fuck. The midget had no sooner sat his little body on the couch when Sarah grabbed his Bible and pamphlets out of his tiny hands and started kissing his almost normal-size face like the Rapture was just around the corner. Story is the midget never went back to his church after Sarah was through with him. It's said he's on TV some nights, wrestling other midgets. Entertainment, some call it.

I've heard it said that Sarah's mom came home to find Sarah holding the midget over her and plunging his body up and down between her spread legs and moaning something awful. The midget, by this time having given up shouting scripture at Sarah, was making noises Sarah's mom told her hair dresser sounded like some kind of barnyard animal in full rut. She grabbed the midget out of Sarah's grasp and pulled him up and out of her, and that midget shot his load all over her best visiting dress, not to mention the couch and the rug. Some even got on the dog, I've heard it said. Heard Sarah's mom told her hair dresser she wouldn't have thought such a small body could make so much of the stuff, was how she put it. It's said to this day no Jehovah's Witness will ring the doorbell where Sarah's mom still lives, that they hurry right past the house and won't even come up to the porch to so much as leave a pamphlet.

"I suppose, Leroy," Jackson shouts back, "you won't settle for nothing less than a virgin?" Leroy's face, though I can't see it from the back seat, must be doing some real acrobatics with that. Jackson knows it riles Leroy any time anyone uses that word. Virgin. Seeing as how Leroy claims he still is one. Leroy actually growls, and Jackson, he shifts more toward the window he threw the bottle out and hunches down a bit in his seat till the growling stops.

All those women I've witnessed in his waiting room lusting after Leroy makes it hard for me to believe Leroy ain't had none, though I've never caught Leroy in a lie about anything else, so I guess I have to give weight to his claim. One thing I do know is, he never had Sarah. One night as she was pulling things back on in the back seat of my Pinto, she told me she'd been after Leroy for as long as she could remember and that he was one guy she just couldn't figure.

"A guy who says no," she asked me as I was buckling up my belt, "I mean, what's he saving himself for? He don't like guys, does he?" she asked.

I told her that as far as I knew he didn't, which was the truth. And I've known Leroy as long as anyone I guess, even Jackson.

"Then I don't get it," she said. "I mean, the other night I waited till after you had locked up the front on your way out, and then I slipped in one of the back windows and got naked and snuck up behind him and started rubbing myself against him, and you know what he did?"

I shook my head, starting to get a little excited again, which surprised me. It usually takes over an hour after Sarah's through with me. She is one thorough woman.

"He yelped and pushed me back," she said, "and grabbed a filthy tarp and threw it over me before picking me up and carrying me to the back door where he set me out, closed the door and locked it. Then he opened the window I'd climbed in and threw my clothes at me before locking the window too." Sarah getting her clothes back on in that alley was something a lot of folks in town would have paid to see, but, according to Sarah, Leroy just turned from the locked window and walked off and was swallowed up by the dark inside.

"Well," Sarah said, "I can take a hint as good as the next girl. That Leroy, he ain't never gonna get another shot at this." Sarah pointing at her damp crotch—her panties and shorts still in a bundle on the floor—was too much, and we ended up going at it again.

"Look Jackson," Leroy yells. The engine might as well be remembering a time Sarah was straddling it, what with all the noise it's making and all the shaking it's up to. It's hard, I know, not being loud with Sarah.

Once we were hiding in the back row of the choir loft, in the one section that's half-hidden by some of the organ's pipes. It was an Ash Wednesday, and Sarah, who had the sweetest soprano voice one could imagine when she sang, the purity in that singing voice of hers no doubt the work of some imp or demon, a sort of inside joke between God and the devil, had said that the way the preacher touched that cross of ash to her forehead had really got her going and she couldn't wait, which is why we were in the back row. The few other dedicated choir members there for a service in the middle of the week, a skeleton crew you might say, were all in the first row of the loft, and, when they got out to go get in line for the ashes on their foreheads, Sarah's hand scuttled under my choir robes and got me going, too, before she lifted her robes—she had nothing on under them—and sat on me so I was inside her almost before I knew what was happening. As she wriggled there on my lap, wriggled and swirled and made other motions I got no words for, she looked back at me over the left shoulder I was imagining without the robes—I always loved the sharp curves of those naked shoulders of hers—and whispered to me, sternly, not to make any noise. "Stay quiet," she whispered, and then she faced the preacher who was still at the altar touching ash to the foreheads of kneeling choir members and other parishioners. I suppose if it had been anyone other than Sarah I'd have been a bit bothered by how clear it was that, in her mind, Sarah was backward-straddling the preacher and it was his ash-covered hands gripping her hips and not mine. But with Sarah there was never much use to the bother of jealousy. Sarah wouldn't truck with it none.

And the thing was, there was no room for jealousy in that choir loft. I mean, it was me Sarah was sitting on and it was me trying desperately not to start up with the animal sounds she always pulled out of me in my truck or down by the creek at night. Though I suspected, even as Sarah swallowed a little whimper in her throat and then whispered to me to go on and finish, that the preacher had made some monkey sounds of his own with Sarah. That he had, like me, felt just like the wilted violin pinched between the fingers of the naked woman in that painting by Dali about cruelty or something like it. The afternoon our teacher projected that slide on the ripped screen in our Art Appreciation class was the day Sarah first led me off to the storage room she had found in the basement. There, surrounded by busted up harps and cellos and the remnants of volleyball nets and some things I never took the time to figure out what they'd been, Sarah got naked and set out to teach me how to touch her and what it meant to be touched by a girl who knew more about a man's body than any man could know. A few hours later, when I saw that Dali painting, I didn't listen to the teacher rattle off her usual psycho babble to *explain* the painting. I knew just exactly how that violin felt, hanging there wilted in front of that peeling tower. And the nakedness of that woman's torso in the window didn't come close to how naked Sarah had just been in that dim room surrounded by cast-off, misused things.

"All I'm saying is," Leroy yells to Jackson, "she don't seem the type to commit to one guy, you know?" I know. Leroy is wrong. When Sarah's with you, she's with you and there's no one else. She commits to every guy she's with. Though I don't know, it might be more accurate to say that she commits to the act. That seems wrong, though; that seems to somehow lessen or cheapen what it is Sarah does. Sarah commits to the moment, maybe that's it. Maybe it's as simple as that. That Sarah's more alive in any moment than most people could be said to have really lived in their entire lives.

Maybe that's why Sarah was the best person to have been with me when I saw that body hanging in the oak alongside Route 7. That's what wrecked my car. I mean, it's not every day you see a naked dead man hanging from a tree just off the road. Sarah and me were on our way back to town after a little excursion. That's what Sarah called them, our *excursions into the natural world*, and we were both singing along with Lynyrd Skynyrd and the live version of "Free Bird." Sarah's heart-breakingly perfect soprano voice did amazing things with that "Bye, bye babe, it's been a sweet love," especially with her warm hand stroking my thigh. I had stopped trying to sing and was just listening to Sarah's sweet voice overwhelm the somewhat tinny voice coming out of the radio, and just as she sang "cause the Lord knows I'm to blame" we came around a bend and I saw the corpse hanging from that oak and lost control of the car and slammed into the next oak over. Luckily I hit the brakes before we hit the tree, so neither of us were more than banged up. Heck, the next day I was more sore from our excursion than from crashing into the tree.

Sarah got out first. It wasn't so much that I was dazed from my Pinto smashing into the tree and my head colliding with the windshield, though I suppose I was dazed. It was more that I wasn't so eager to have to deal with what was hanging out there. The dead guy. His name was Zachary, the paper said the next day. He was the estranged—that was the word the newspaper used—brother of some traveling faith healer. As I recall, the paper said the guy, this Phineas, swallowed some kind of worms as part of a ritual meant to cleanse people of their sins. Seems some folks will do just about anything for salvation.

The radio was still going. Guess I hadn't turned the ignition off completely and juice was still getting to it. I remember sitting there and, as Lynyrd Skynyrd's guitars wailed into sounds that just felt like they had to break free of whatever it was that was holding them back, watching Sarah through the windshield, which was now cracked so that there was this refracted light that seemed to want to embrace Sarah, or pierce her maybe. My seat belt was still holding me in. Sarah walked right up to the dead man. Even from inside the car I could see this dead man had one hell of a boner. I'd always heard blood rushes to the extremities at death, so I guessed that's what it was, and not that Sarah, this beautiful young woman, was walking up to where he was hanging from the tree. "Free Bird" was all I could hear, but I could see Sarah was saying something as she approached the corpse. A second skin of flies rose off the body as Sarah got closer, and to this day I can still imagine that sad insect drone rising from the silent flesh and Sarah's lilting voice murmuring just under the murmur of the flies. Though even imagining it, I can't hear what Sarah's saying, what she said, to the dead man hanging there all full of lust even in death.

When I do remember it, and imagine it, it's always with the sound of longing captured by the whine of electric guitars as soundtrack, and the light is that kind of muted light that makes the figures it caresses seem almost too real, and it's always in slow motion. Sarah walks right up to the dead man and starts rubbing his feet. She's looking up into his face and it's clear she's saying something to him, and it almost seems as if he's listening, like he's leaning his head down to better hear what she's saying as she rubs his feet.

It's what happens next I can't shake. "Lord knows I can't cha-a-a-ange" is coming over the radio, and outside Sarah's hands move up the dead man's naked thighs until they are grasping his hard-on, and, as the guitars go back into their heart-breaking wails—that music so full of a longing for re-lease that every teenage boy can't help but try to imitate it with whatever voice he can muster—Sarah's stroking with both hands what seems now, in memory, to be a massive erection. It doesn't at first seem wrong that this gets me hard too, even though Sarah looks like some sort of angel out there in that surreal light. And then the dead man's balls let loose and empty themselves all over Sarah who's just standing there, one hand stroking the still-erect cock and the other, which had to have been just dripping with the dead man's spunk, in her mouth. When she turns to look back at me in the car, one hand's holding onto the dead man's cock and the other's in her mouth and, as she pulls her hand out of her mouth, she's smiling, and there's this light around her—no doubt due to the refraction caused by the cracks in the windshield—that is just the most beautiful light I've ever seen in my life. It has the quality of the light that comes through the stained glass windows in church, that kind of feeling of time and meaning being a part of the light.

It was that light that wilted my boner. This was nothing sordid, was what that light told me. This was beyond my understanding. This was holy, is what the light said.

The memory, oddly, never makes it past that moment with that unreal light surrounding Sarah with that crazy smile on her face. How we got back or who we told about the dead man, though I'm sure neither of us told what Sarah had done to the dead man's boner, that's all pretty much a blank. The Pinto never ran again, and Sarah and I never went on another excursion. Of any sort. Anywhere. In fact, since our encounter with the dead man hanging by the road the only guy Sarah's been with, as far as anyone knows, is Jackson. Lucky guy, that Jackson.

"Look, Leroy," Jackson yells over the engine, which is sounding more like what I imagine flies grown to gigantic size from exposure to radiation—like in those fifties monster movies—would sound like as they settled over the houses and shops in town than like any human or animal sound arising out of passion. "You might as well just give up. Me and Sarah, we're in love and we're going to get hitched. In the church and everything. All I'm asking is, Leroy, are you going to be my best man or not?"

Leroy's eyes in the rear view mirror don't so much look sad or even worried as they look trapped. I doubt Leroy knows Sarah told me about the night he threw her naked out of the shop, but it's my guess that night is what's going through Leroy's head.

"Of course Leroy'll be your best man, Jackson," I yell from the back seat. "How could he let anyone else stand up there with you?" Yelling, for the most part, keeps my stutter in check.

Leroy looks like he's chewing on a little cud of his own. Then you can see the surrender in him and he nods. "Sure, Jackson, sure," Leroy says in a way that makes it clear he's given in and will do it. "But why do you got to do it so soon?" he yells, pulling into his shop's parking lot and cutting the engine. The memory of all that mechanical noise—what Leroy claims is the best music he knows—keeps us hearing the engine for a bit.

With Jackson's head turned toward Leroy as it is just now I can see he's smiling. "I don't want my first born to be a bastard like you, that's why," he says.

Though I can tell he wants to, Leroy doesn't ask the question anyone who'd grown up with Sarah would think of asking. Leroy doesn't ask, as we're getting out of his car, if Jackson's sure it's his. Leroy just grins and as soon as Jackson's out of the car he grabs him in a bear hug.

I'm glad Jackson believes it's his. And maybe he's right to believe it is. But that's not what I believe. No sir. As far as I'm concerned that baby growing in Sarah is the son of the brother of a faith healer who it's said swallowed worms. It's Zachary's baby Sarah's carrying. That's what I believe cause that makes sense of that miraculous light around Sarah as she swallowed the dead man's spunk. It makes sense of the change in Sarah ever since the night she whacked off a corpse. And I've been in church enough to know things like that happened in the Bible all the time. The Bible's loaded with all kinds of miracle births. Not just Christ's. Hell, even in the Old Testament strange pregnancies were always happening. That's what this is. It's a miracle, and I was there to be witness to it, as the Bible would say. I can give witness. When the time comes, though, for Jackson's sake, I'll just say a prayer and keep my witnessing to myself.

THE UNDER THE RIVERS HUMMING CROSS OF ROME, GEORGIA

Once my name blazoned across a lurid poster stapled to phone poles and taped to storefront windows would have had those seven syllables echoing all over town, like the faint memory of an old lover still imagined some nights slipping into your bed, someone else snoring beside you, to remind you what it was like to have every inch of your skin feel even the slightest caress of breath, your name whispered into your most secret places. Those syllables would've been repeated on the seven hills of this place an actor once called the armpit of America, and it would've seemed a blessing. A local phenom, it was as if just the saying of my name were some chant in a language as old as the stars, and as mysterious. As if saying my name could make things possible, things folks believed they wanted to be possible.

Back then, people remembered my father and, reading my name, thought of him. It was my father they were still coming to see, in the person of his son, the closest any of them could get to him anymore.

My father'd been the real thing till the dementia took him. The room he rots in isn't a place folks would want to take their kids. I used to think some magic could be possible there, but doubt is a part of any true faith. Something my father taught me.

I'm a magician, part of a dying breed in this overly secular, technological age, and a poser at that. My father, though he performed feats of magic folks said were nothing short of miracles, was no magician. He was a preacher. From the old school. At times he preached with faith healers. Other times ordinary folks, listening to him under some filthy, ragged canvas tent raised in some mundane park in the center of a town or in a fallow field on the edge of some borough or other, would all of a sudden take to speaking in tongues and my father would listen and translate the gibberish coming out of the twisted and twisting mouth of the afflicted man or woman, and the message would always turn out to be one of redemption, of salvation through the word of God he always held in his right hand. He never let go of that Bible as he ranted and sang and translated under a smudged and sooty canvas sky. He never opened it neither. Didn't have to. The whole of it was a part of him. He could recite any passage and, at times, despite being his son and so knowing him in ways the congregations he challenged to live their faith could not, he even had me thinking I could see the angels he said were always with us, watching over us, keeping possible the connection between the creator and those he had formed out of the dust of the earth.

When I visit him now he almost never has anything to say that he'll say loud enough for me to hear. Fragments that sound like they could be from the Bible said mostly to the barren wall that glares on one side of his hospital bed and an almost musical, incoherent mumbling, these comprise my father's vocabulary now. It could be what's left of my father is trying to chant his way back out of the dementia to the world he so loved.

The nurses all know he was a man of faith. One of the night nurses, Gwen is the name on the tag she wears, has told me, whispering as she turns my father's body to prevent bedsores, that she had gone to hear him one night under a tent in the town's park and had found herself speaking in some language she didn't know. She said my father had translated her rantings into a beautiful Bible verse about how love is God's greatest gift and how it can reshape this world and all our lives as we rush about in our sorrow and our despair. She's told me that night changed everything for her, and she owes all the caring for others she's accomplished in her adult years as a nurse to that moment in that dusty tent with my father telling her and the whole congregation what God was saying through her.

"It's like," Gwen told me one night as she was emptying my father's bedpan, "all my caring for the injured and the hurt and all those in pain has been God telling all those folks, in the midst of their grief and their suffering, God loves the world. That's the point, you know, of his son dying on the cross and all. God so loves this world and those of us who live in it that he's willing to take on our suffering, to share it, to be a father who loses a son, in order to let us all know we are loved. Each night I tend to my charges I'm reminding them God loves them."

Every time I hear someone talk like this, especially someone touched by my father's words into believing such things, I don't know whether to curse the God they believe loves us or to just shake my head and walk away. From it all. From the believer, from my father, from his God, from this world his God supposedly loves so much.

Some nights I sit beside my father while he mumbles under the clean bedsheets Gwen or some other nurse who seems to adore him has just wrapped him in after taking away the soiled ones. He mumbles musically in a barely audible whisper, not much more than a humming, and I want to get right up in his gnarled face. Father, I'd say, tell me the trick. Religion, I'd say, though I know if he could hear and understand it how much it would hurt him, is the greatest magic trick of all. Teach me that trick, father.

I don't do it, of course. Not just because I know he's too far gone from this world and his life in it to be able to give me an answer even if there were one. I don't ask because I don't want that kind of responsibility. Such magic, I've learned, is a terrible burden. And I want no truck with it, none at all. Sometimes I think it's that burden, and not the Alzheimer's rotting out his brain, that has brought my father to this.

It's a terrible shame that the emissary from the other Rome, the one that gave this town the replica of the sculpture of Romulus and Remus suckling under the she-wolf, in looking for my father, found me instead. My father, he could have handled things better. Of that I have no doubt.

Nor, I'm sure, does Gwen, who changes my father's sheets and turns his frail body several times a night to try to keep it from the pain of those sores, who washes his body with a sponge and a tenderness that has left me weeping. I swear there've been nights I've walked in on her finishing up her ministrations, and seeing her holding his body so limp and trembling with pain in her nurses' arms in the single light over his bed left on at night that seems almost an aura coming from their two bodies in that moment, in that posture, all I can think is that here's a more perfect rendition of the pieta than any sculptor has ever or could ever form out of stone or wood or even clay. And though I may not be a particularly religious man, I know the images. My father collected prints of all his favorite religious art—paintings, sculptures, murals, all of it—and hung those prints on the walls in every room in our house. Most of his favorites were either pietas, where the mother grieves her dead son in her arms, or images of the baby Jesus held by Mary. Not having any memories of my mother holding me, those made me sadder than the pietas.

Art and me, we've always had a complex relationship.

Nights my father had too much of the wrong kind of alcohol and was acting more like the Old Testament God than the God of love he preached about, those nights his fists found the sore of my back for some injustice he was sure I was guilty of, I'd run from the house and head downtown and hunker under that rough she-wolf, trying to find some milk neither Romulus nor Remus had finished off with all their suckling. Those nights I wasn't my father's son. I was another son of Ares, God of War, Romulac, the third twin, the one thought dead at birth who lived on without anyone's notice. I'd heard the stories in school. The myths. And I knew enough to know great myths always leave room for additions, for new narrative directions, so I made up myths those nights and they comforted me.

If I were to take Gwen in my arms some night, there beside what's left of my father in that bed, if I were to tell Gwen about those nights and the myths I made up and of the comfort they offered me, would that rouse my father out of the realm where his disease or his burden or both have taken him? Would he come back to us, come back to me, enough to tell me the trick?

Rosa, my lover, is a gypsy fortune-teller in our little carnival set up every summer in Heritage Park, along the Coosa River. She tells me she can't believe how gullible I can be. "You're a magician, for God's sake," she has said. "Of all people, how can you be bothered by this? Surely you don't believe what he gave you really is one of Christ's fingers?"

How can I explain my lack of doubt about this to Rosa when it makes absolutely no sense to me? But the emissary, he was convincing. His faith remained like an aura around the finger.

The holy relic, he called it. I'd expected a dusty, frail remnant of what wasn't even recognizable as ever having had blood coursing through it. Not this pristine, yet roughly severed, finger.

It was this he had risked everything for. To keep Christ's finger out of the wrong hands, he said. There were factions in the Church. He told me how the Pope had selected him as the only person he could trust. How the Pope explained a story would be concocted of the theft of the finger, but that no shame would befall the emissary. It was his task to get this holy relic to the man those in the Vatican had decided it must go to. My father.

Yes, even the elite in the elder Rome had heard of what my father had done in Rome, Georgia, and it was word of the miracle of the three rivers that had persuaded the Pope to send his man to Georgia to find my father and to hand the holy relic over into his care. Too bad they waited as long as they did before acting. By the time the emissary of the Pope arrived, the disease had taken my father and left in his stead a dementia-encrusted shell of the man he had been.

The emissary had found me here in Rome, Georgia because of the posters all over town for the spring carnival. My name featured prominently on those posters. I had acquired some regional fame for magic, something I had taken up in my youth but studied in private until my father started to decline. Not that any of my tricks or illusions come close to the things my father did with his congregation every night under that tent. My father had the power of a belief system and the longing for faith in every human heart to fall back on. All I and my ilk have to rely on is the desire to be entertained. Some of us get a lot out of that, though. Enough to earn a living. Me and Rosa, we make out pretty well, each in our own way.

Rosa's name on those posters was second in size only to mine. Though she was in fact not of true gypsy lineage, she had lived a gypsy lifestyle for years in Atlanta before necessity and fate brought her to this place. She fell in with some carnies and found she had a talent for reading people. "If I get in the right mood, and the candles and scarves and the crystal ball reflecting those candles seems to help get me there, it's almost like I can hear them whispering to me what it is they want or need to hear from me. So I tell them," she says, and laughs. "And they give me money and thank me for telling them just what they asked to hear." Of course it doesn't hurt that Rosa is a remarkably gorgeous woman. Beauty tends to be able to put us in a place it's difficult to explain anything from.

Rosa doesn't see it. Her beauty, I mean. Once when I was gazing at her face and thinking if there were female archangels they must look like this, Rosa told me she hated how one of her nostrils was bigger than the other. "It always makes me worry," she said, "that when someone's looking at me all they're thinking is, Oh my God, how can she live with such a deformity?" Rosa is a show person to the core, but about this she's absolutely serious.

When Rosa led the emissary into my little theater, she kept one of her delicate hands flitting in front of her nose so he wouldn't have the chance to notice.

I still remember how for weeks the marquee at the movie house had ignored the titles of whatever movies were being watched in the dark by people who put too much butter on their popcorn and tried to forget there was a world out there they had to go back to. Rather than touting the titles of the movies showing, for two weeks in big black and bold letters it proclaimed, "Preacher Promises Feat of Faith of Biblical Proportions." Under this was a date and a time. That was it. For weeks people paid their money and had to ask the girl who handed them their tickets what they had just paid to see. Those of us who were fifteen and knew the secret of the side door that wouldn't shut all the way snuck in without knowing what we were sneaking in to see.

I knew something of what was coming. My father had given me a role to play in what was to be his greatest demonstration of the power of faith to transform the world. That's how he spoke of it, when he did speak of it. Which wasn't often. During the weeks leading up to the miracle, my father spent almost every waking hour praying. Sometimes others of his flock came to our house and prayed with my father. Other times my father prayed alone. Some nights he asked me to kneel and pray with him, and I did, even though I didn't really believe for sure in his God and had no idea most of the time what my father was saying in his prayers. Those weeks it was always Latin he prayed in. I knew how Latin sounded but in those days I knew very little what it meant.

It was during one of our praying bouts that my father told me what was to be my role in this drama of his. He told me he was going to separate the Etowah, the Oostanaula, and the Coosa. "Going to pull them apart," my father said, "and hold them at bay." While my father held the waters of the three rivers at bay with the power of his faith and the prayers of his followers, I was to lead a procession of worshippers down into the river beds, and, at the center of where the rivers come together, I would place a metal cross. He held the cross out to me. It reflected the dim light of the candles in that mostly darkened room and for a moment it almost had the look of flesh. A cross of flesh, I thought. I was to bury a cross of flesh in the fish-flapping bed of three conjoined rivers. I wasn't sure if I would have laughed or cried had I been able to let anything out at that moment. Whichever it would have been, I held it in for my father's sake. Out of respect, I guess. I didn't want to risk taking anything else meaningful away from him. I'd already taken so much from him, I knew. Though my father always maintained the lie he told me about how my mother died, by fifteen I had found the obituary my father had clipped from the local paper and hidden telling how my mother had died giving birth to me.

The day of the miracle I stood with my father on the Second Avenue bridge and prayed with him and the hundreds of men and women and children in the gathered crowd. I don't think my father had slept for several days. He had a look about him of distance. It could take years, I remember thinking as I stood there right beside him, to get to where he is now. It was likely, I figured, I'd never reach him no matter how far I walked.

There wasn't a cloud in sight and not even a suggestion of so much as a breeze. The world had gone still. Standing there reciting the words my father had taught me for the occasion, I started to become aware of the absolute silence the words being uttered by my father and by me and by the men, women, and children gathered along that bridge and in the streets of Rome, Georgia, fell into. For just a moment I thought I could hear the sounds of suckling, and I thought of the sculpture of Romulus and Remus and their she-wolf mother, and, though my father was stone sober and reverent, part of me wanted to hunker through that crowd and crawl up under the she-wolf and go after what my brothers were getting, there without me.

What I had been hearing, though, turned out not to be suckling at all. As the sound got louder, it became clear it was coming from below the surface of the three rivers. My father's voice was no longer familiar. The words he was shouting at the waters all around us were no language I had ever heard. To this day I'm not sure it was language that was coming out of my father at that moment. It might have been the pure and dynamic utterance of faith, something always beyond any and all languages spoken and written down by men.

Children were pointing at the rivers with the little leaf-woven crosses their tiny hands clutched. Who it was who had made and handed out those crosses I never found out. A choir started up with some hymn I didn't recognize. Whatever hymn it was, it was a beautiful sound there between the almost-silence of the world and the praying of the crowd and the shouting of my father. The metal cross I held in both my hands started to hum along with the hymn the choir sang. Even the sky seemed to be humming, and the mud hens passing by below us on driftwood seemed to have tuned their song to our music.

It wasn't until the mud hens rose off the driftwood that I noticed what had started to happen to the waters below. They were receding. It was as if the flow of the rivers had sped up in three different directions, so that where the rivers merged the level of the waters kept going down. Things long submerged were becoming visible. The pickup truck Gabriel Watkins had driven off the bridge one night drunk, for example. Everyone had said it was a miracle he was able to get out and swim to a bank of the Etowah, crawl out of the river and stumble home soaking wet. As the waters receded, more and more things people had lost to the rivers or had asked the rivers to hide for them came uncovered. There were baby carriages and a crib or two. A twisted-up and rusted bed frame seemed almost a curse in the mud. And what must have once been a child's swing set creaked in the damp air, like some kind of warning bell.

As the river bed itself emerged, leaving fish that hadn't been fast enough to keep up with the sped-up current flapping with a sick sucking sound in mud, more intimate items could be seen. Most folks turned away from the sight of the detritus of their lives stuck in the mud of the river beds. What they saw by looking away from where the water had left was where it had gone.

What must have been fifty yards or so down each river was a roiling wall of water. Now and then a fish plopped through the wall of water and fell to the mud of the river bed where seconds before the water had been. My father had done it. Or his faith had. Or the faith everyone had in my father. Whatever it was that had done it, the rivers were parted. No trick some magician performed on a stage with props and a lovely assistant could come close. The roiling walls of water seemed to shimmer in time with the song the crowd was joining the choir in singing. What they were singing was my processional.

In the robes my father had dressed me in that morning, I started down the embankment toward the mud flats where the water had been minutes before, the air down there so damp it was almost like breathing honey. Everything felt slowed down somehow. The choir, singing, followed me. Above us, on the bridge, I could make out the barely recognizable voice of my father still chanting. Years later I would wonder if what had been coming forth out of my father's throat had been the unrepeatable, unknowable names of God, but by then my father was mumbling incoherencies in a damp bed, tended to by uniformed women who offered him what grace they had to offer because they remembered who he had been, or had been told who he had been, that he had been the preacher who parted the rivers so his son could step down into the place where the rivers came together and plant a cross of metal that hummed.

Gwen had hugged me the first time I visited my father on her shift. She had been a young woman in the choir that day my father parted the rivers, and she remembered slogging behind me through that mud, stepping over busted picture frames, the photos they'd held long since dissolved away, mud-encrusted beer bottles, what must have been the ripped-off arms of easy chairs, and all the rest. Gwen remembers to this day how the choir's singing seemed to hang loose in the damp air around us. She remembers looking at the three roiling walls of river water and thinking how beautiful that water, subdued by my father's faith, had seemed, and how the water seemed to shimmer with the hymns they were singing. And Gwen remembers how, when I sank that cross into the mud where the three rivers come together, that cross took up the hymn the choir was singing. Sometimes, she's told me, when she's alone with my father at night she whispers the story in his ear. She's told me he smiles as she tells him of the singing cross at the bottom of the rivers. At times, she's said, the story seems to bring my father some sort of peace. "Once," Gwen told me, "he stopped that mumbling he does and started singing." Gwen swears it was the song the choir was singing, the hymn the cross took up and kept singing as we made our way back up to the bridge where my father smiled at me and went silent as the waters of the rivers rushed back together over that singing cross.

When I brought the emissary of the Pope to see my father, Gwen kissed his hand and started to tell him the story of the singing cross under the river. The emissary of the Pope stopped her, blessed her, and told her he needed to be alone with my father and me. He had an authority about him, is the only way I can say it. Gwen nodded to me as she left the room, as if she meant to offer me some solace.

The Pope's emissary leaned over my father's bed to listen to what my father was mumbling, the nonsense that had been all he had left of language for some time. It was night and the patients were all meant to be asleep, so the only light in the room was from the single-bulb lamp at the head of my father's hospital bed. My father and the emissary of the Pope were framed by that light. It was, I thought, as if Caravaggio had painted the moment, and the sacredness of that light made me feel like a voyeur, like I didn't belong there. It didn't matter that it was *my* father, or what was left of him, in that bed the emissary leaned over, listening. It didn't matter that I was the only living relative of the frail, mumbling man in that hospital bed. Especially when the emissary, still leaning over my father, whispered to him what had the feel of a question, I felt like an intruder.

Until my father stopped his mumbling and spoke my name and pointed to me. The emissary said "Him?" with what was obviously doubt, but my father, no longer mumbling at all and with a lucidity to his face and his form I had almost forgotten he could command, said loud enough I could hear, "Give the relic to my son. He will find the person who should be its keeper until the time comes for it to end up where it needs to end up, in a more primordial world than that of men." It was my father's voice, a voice I hadn't heard for so long that I had almost lost the memory of its sound.

Before I could ask my father anything, and there were things I wanted to ask him I'd been saving up for some time, he was gone, back into his incoherent mumbling, all lucidity gone from his voice and his form. The emissary of the Pope held out his hand to me and in his hand was an ornately engraved box made of wood and what looked to be some sort of pearl. It could have been a pen and pencil set—that was the size of it. I confess I sold that ornate little box to an art dealer for a decent sum of money, enough to buy some new props for my act and some nice things for Rosa. Rosa called that money my retainer, my fee for acting as an agent for the Vatican in Georgia in regards to the contents of the box, which was, the emissary swore, "the severed middle finger off the right hand of our savior Jesus Christ." That was how he put it. And to this day I have no doubt that what was in that box was in fact one of Christ's fingers.

Faith, it's said, is what you have when you believe without proof. If that's so, then it's not fair to say that I have faith the finger was the finger of Jesus Christ. From the day the emissary handed me that ornate box, kissed me on both cheeks and walked out of the room where my father had returned to mumbling music in his hospital bed, and headed back, I assume, to that other Rome, things have conspired to convince me of the authenticity of that finger.

First it was the dreams. That very night, after Rosa and I had examined the finger a bit before closing the box and putting it away in the drawer of the nightstand by the bed, I drifted off to sleep listening, as was my custom, to Rosa's soft sleep-breathing beside me. By the time I woke up in the morning, I wasn't sure I would ever let myself go to sleep again.

My dreams, nightmares I should say, were haunted by scenes of horrible suffering and despair, and I felt every bit of misery experienced by all the varied grotesque figures in those scenes. When a gator tore a woman to pieces in some swamp and swallowed her torso, with her head, her lovely mouth still open in a scream, still attached and whole, my bones ached with every grinding of gator tooth on bone. It was *my* body that gator tore asunder and swallowed. It was my mouth still trying to scream as it filled with the blood and bile of that ancient reptile.

When a broken-down shack on fire collapsed around a bruised and battered figure of a man, my flesh caught fire and started to turn to ash as every nerve ending under my skin lit up with such pain it seemed as if my body itself were nothing but a scream.

When a woman ravaged by despair jumped from a bridge to the river below, it was my body hitting the water and going under and drifting and drifting until the current wore my flesh away and drew my bones apart and out to sea. This was the worst. Since the miracle of the three rivers, when I had stood at the juncture of the rivers and planted a metal cross that sang in the mud of the river bed and watched the waters, released, crash back and engulf that cross and the place I had just been standing, I have been terrified by any large body of water. The worst being rivers.

But the dreams and the fear of sleep they brought me were not the only proof. Things started to happen during my act, strange things. Things that weren't supposed to happen. Like when the scarf pushed into my fist that's supposed to transform into the dove with the opening of the fist became, instead, a gecko that crawled down my arm and leapt onto the neck of my assistant who screamed, and the gecko slipped into her mouth stifling her scream, and when she opened her mouth again the dove flew out of her mouth and landed on her hand. The crowd loved it and applauded like crazy.

Or when I made my assistant disappear, and rather than finding her, like I should have, when I opened the box a second time, huge reeds, like those that frolic along the banks of the three rivers, burst out like they'd been stuffed in there and just kept growing till they could break the box open themselves. When the reeds burst out of the box there was a faint music they made as they swayed there on stage, and it was the tune my assistant was whistling as she came up behind me out of nowhere and put her arms around me and the crowd went wild.

My reputation was growing, but chaos is not something a magician feels comfortable with. A magician is supposed to know what's about to happen, and what happens is supposed to be what he expects to happen. Trying to play off of chaos will put any magician on edge.

"It's that damn finger," I told Rosa as we held one another and our breathing settled down after making love. I loved how Rosa had her luscious mouth open, trying not to breathe through her nose. I remember her saying once she thought her breathing sounded off due to the one nostril being so much larger than the other. Not that I could see this difference in her nostrils, and to me her breathing was always in perfect pitch.

"Maybe it is," she said, which surprised me. Rosa had not bought into the notion that the finger might be authentic. "Today something happened I'm not sure what to make of." Rosa sounded scared. I rubbed her shoulders and my right hand made its way down her lower back, rubbing, and on down. She has said me rubbing her butt makes her feel safe. "This old guy came in to my tent for a reading. I could tell right off he was missing someone," Rosa said, "and whoever it was their absence was a terrible presence he couldn't escape. So I guessed it was his wife he was missing and he told me it was, that she had gotten sick with something the doctors didn't have a name for, much less a treatment for or a cure, and she had died in his arms a little more than a month ago. He said he just needed to know she was with God. That, and that she hadn't, in dying, forgotten him or that he loved her. I don't know why," Rosa said, "but this guy really got to me. His grief was so genuine and palpable. He made me feel his sadness." This was unusual. It took a lot to get to Rosa. A certain ability to maintain a distance between you and others is something every gypsy seer relies on, and Rosa had it in spades.

Damn that finger. I had to get rid of it, to give it to whoever was supposed to have it.

"The thing is," Rosa said, "as I started my chanting into the crystal ball and my breathing over the candles to get the flames doing their little dances, making the air in the tent itself seem alive, I heard a woman's voice in the distance, getting closer." Rosa's entire body shivered as she told me about the voice, and not even my warm hand on her lovely butt helped. "The voice," Rosa said, "it was getting closer, and then I could see the old guy was hearing it, too. The look on his face told me all I needed to know. The voice both of us were hearing was the voice of his dead wife. This was happening, for real. This guy so loved his wife that his longing to speak to her through me had actually brought her out of the grave to talk." Rosa had curled up in a compact, fetal curl against my stomach and had pulled the sheets around her like they were some kind of crazy shroud. She was terrified just telling the story.

Rosa is very convincing with her act, but like my act Rosa's had always been all illusion. A trick, or rather a collection of tricks that, put together in the right sequence with the right tone, had been enough to gain her a certain amount of what we in the business call name recognition. It had to be the finger that was making everything real.

"So I sat there and pretended to be focusing so as not to lose the contact with his dead wife," Rosa told me, her voice muffled a bit by the sheets that were up over her face, "and I listened to the two of them talk to one another about their daily routines as if there wasn't something called death and the wife had just been off visiting relatives for a few days. These two people, you see," Rosa's muffled voice sounded even stranger, "they loved one another. Get it? Real, unquestionable and unquestioning love. I've never been more terrified."

I got the details on the old guy from Rosa, including where he stopped every morning for his coffee and biscuit. A diner where the waitress, who remembers the two of them, him and his wife, holding hands around their coffee cups and how the wife used to put butter and honey on her husband's biscuit for him, cuts his biscuit in half for him every morning and spreads it with butter and honey just as the wife had.

"When he told his dead wife how the waitress does that for him every morning," Rosa said, and it was clear she was trying not to cry, "I swear I heard a little sniffle, like, though she was dead, she just had to cry at that."

When the old guy came in the diner, I knew, even before the waitress walked over to him with a pot of coffee in her right hand ready to pour, that it was him. Rosa had pegged him fine. The finger was in my pocket, wrapped up in a pale blue dish towel. It almost felt warm there in my pocket.

I told him Rosa and I were a couple and how she'd been impressed with his love for his departed wife. That she had told me how pure and inspiring his love for her was. I told him the story of the emissary coming from his Rome to our Rome looking for my father and finding me instead. I told him I had been charged with finding the person who could be trusted to care for the finger. I tried to imagine how that must have sounded, a magician in a diner talking about caring for the finger of Jesus Christ. I wasn't certain that even every single ounce of my stage charm, my presence, would be enough to persuade the old guy to take the finger from me.

"My wife," the old guy said, "after I left your Rosa in her tent and was walking home, she told me you'd be here this morning. She told me to listen to what you had to say, cause you had to say it, and to agree to take care of the finger." I put the dish towel with its bit of flesh in the hand of this old guy who so loved his wife she couldn't stay quiet being dead. He nodded and winked once, and I left him there to eat his biscuit with butter and honey in peace.

Tonight, Rosa and I got as naked as we could and ravished each other. I made tulips appear and then turned them into a silk scarf Rosa wrapped around her beautiful throat and let dangle over her belly.

"Any voices today, my dear?" I said as I started to make that scarf do a provocative little dance between her thighs.

"Nary a one. God, I love any day the dead stay dead and all I have to do is fake it." I gave Rosa my best hurt face and she laughed and covered me with her body and the silk scarf draped over the both of us.

Asleep, I stand on a bridge next to my father who is dressed in a tuxedo and is fanning out a deck of cards and telling a woman whose face I can't see to pick one, any one.

Then my father's frail body is draped with white sheets and he is mumbling. I try to say something to him, to ask him what he's doing out here on this bridge on such a cold night, but I'm mute. The best I can do is put my arms around my father and start to hum some hymn I've heard him sing with his congregation a thousand times. None of the words come to me. All I can do is hum the tune. The same tune comes from below us in the dark, where I know three rivers flow into and out of one another, and where a metal cross planted there by the son of a holy man hums as it holds together, or so I want, in the dream, to believe, three rivers and a father and a son.

OLD TIME RELIGION

We knew Clifford liked to look. We didn't think it hurt anyone. If we had known what he'd done to those geese back in the woods, we'd have kept him away from Maggie.

You must have seen the pictures of the geese. For days the local paper ran the polaroids found in his room, the death masks of tortured water birds. We've imagined the wings, shamed by the words carved into them in anger, wanted to fly back to a country cold enough to deaden the scream of a woman as a knife carved words across her back muscles, words from the Bible about absent angels.

There's no doubt he was sick. His mother left him locked for days at a time in a room without windows. We all knew it, whether or not it's true. Clifford was one of us. No one doubted that. With his past some hate was natural, but to gouge a woman's flesh, that's too much. We never wanted to imagine that.

But now, thanks to Clifford, we have to imagine Maggie's skin raised into bumps that, for a blind man, might have spelled out some forgotten name of God. We have to imagine Clifford's blind heart sounded like some ragged bird singing hymns in the pale branches of his ribs. We have to imagine Clifford wanted to carve an eloquence out of her flesh he couldn't manage in his speech. That his stammer mimicked the dying geese nailed to trees. We have to imagine everything.

But Clifford did more than imagine. He saw things in bodies that spoke to him, that said they wanted out. That's what the experts say.

We know better. We've lived here, too, among all the crosses that can't keep our flesh from singing long hymns that limp through us, and we recognize the violence within us all that can leave even an angel stammering. What chance do any of us down here have, to see, without imagining, what we are.

A VERY OLD MUSIC

First time I saw Karl he was on his riding mower, and at first I thought he must have his daughter on his lap. Folks round here often do that. Keeps the little imps entertained, or at least distracted, for a spell. If I hadn't had the time to get a better look, that's what I'd have gone away thinking. Just a father keeping his daughter from getting cranky before dinner. But I was walking slow that day—weighted down with burdens no one looking might readily see any sign of—so I was close enough long enough to see, as the sun angled just so through the trees lining the lawn, the truth of it. That here was a man out mowing his lawn who had a second head on his shoulders. A woman's head at that. And though I could see she was saying something in his left ear, it would be awhile before I heard her speak and learned she only spoke Greek. And not modern Greek, but the Greek of Homer, of the Old Testament, a Greek of mystery and faith and everything that goes unwitnessed in this fallen world. A Greek few folks can understand even in Greece itself. Karl had no idea at all what she was saying, but she was almost always saying something in that sore left ear of his. No wonder the man seemed to have a permanent lean to the right.

God sure does like to keep things entertaining. I mean, after all I've witnessed in this world just a walk down an unassuming street can bring me face to face with another enigma, more proof that the miraculous and the tragic are as much a part of this desperate world as the mundane. If a man with a woman's head on his shoulder talking Greek in his left ear isn't sign of God's hand in all this, I don't know what is.

It wasn't Karl's feminine tormentor that brought me to this little town in the middle of nowhere, but the pine woods that make up parts of the Chattahoochee National Park. Pine woods being the best places to find scarlet snakes. Least ways, that's what my reading up on them told me. And Subligna—what folks here call this ramshackle version of a town—sounded like Latin to me, like it was the name of something holy and mysterious. Like faith had to be strong in a place with a name like Subligna.

Faith has always been strong in me but, like a scarlet snake, it has burrowed down into the sandy loam that must be all that remains of my soul, and it only comes out some nights to remind itself of the world it burrowed down to get away from, to convince itself that to stay hidden is best.

My preaching days are over. Can't get up in front of folks and convince them to love God with your own faith burrowed deep within you and fearful of showing itself in the light.

Sometimes, having a whiskey in Marlow's, I stare at Gloria in her waitress get-up looking so much, in the dim light of that tavern, like Rachel, it damn near has me ready to go deep into the Chattahoochee Park to hunt for a gator to feed myself to. But no gator can swallow me enough to cleanse me of my sins, or consume the ghost of the woman who haunts me with her body and her music and that perfect face I held in my hands and kissed one last time in the midst of a gator's guts and the shouting and cries from the congregation. Only the snakes hold out hope for me. If I can hunt down the scarlet snake whose markings spell out the depths of my sins, I can cut off its head and carve it and cook it up with some onions and peppers, and once I've eaten that snake maybe then I'll be able to forgive myself. I'll know that snake when I find it. I'll be able to read my sins in the bands that cross its legless body. This I believe.

It takes a lot of faith to keep going in this world. Karl can attest to that.

We drink together, Karl and me. The woman's head growing from his left shoulder only drinks ouzo. I've seen her knock back over a dozen shots of the licorice-tasting stuff at a sitting. One night not long ago, after the seventh or eighth shot of ouzo, she started singing what must have been some ancient sea chantey. It could have been what that fellow Odysseus heard the sirens sing, him bound to the mast and calling out to his crew to let him go. Their ears stopped up with wax, they couldn't hear him, or the sirens. His own plan. That must have been the worst of his torment—that he had willingly participated in what would deny him his chance to have such incredible longing fulfilled. His body become nothing but desire lashed to the mast. It must have seemed absolute cruelty how his crew ignored his transformation in their midst from a creature of skin and blood and the passing of time to pure emptiness crying out to be filled.

The voice the woman's head sang the untranslatable song in was so lovely everyone in Marlow's stopped what they were doing to listen. Not one of us had any idea what words she was singing, but we all knew how it made us feel. Me, all I could do was think of Rachel playing the organ, how those hands of hers could turn the notes of any hymn into a promise of consolation and repair, of the mystical healing only possible with touch. That woman's head was busy seducing every man and woman within earshot.

I don't know what kept me from grabbing Karl and kissing the lips through which that singing poured. After all, I've already kissed the bodiless head of a woman spilled out of a gator's opened gut, so kissing that singing woman's head on Karl's left shoulder wouldn't have felt so strange at all. Guess the mixing of the music and the whiskey just made it so I couldn't move. Mesmerized is the word for it. Most of us in Marlow's were mesmerized.

That such music stirs up rawer passions don't surprise me none either. One man that night in Marlow's got up on the bar and took out his member and tried to put it in the mouth that music was coming from. Thank the Lord for Russell, the bouncer, who knocked the drunk off the bar and dragged him to the door and out into the street. Russ left him there crumpled in a heap of bawling flesh. Course, it's not like some of the rest of us hadn't had the same thought. That music made those lips a promise of such pleasure it was remarkable more of us weren't thrown out that night.

Other nights—and tonight's one of those—the ouzo makes the Greek-speaking woman's head go quiet. Karl gets this smile on his face when this happens and has been known to buy a round for everyone in the place. Not tonight, though. Tonight he just smiles and sips his whiskey and sneaks looks at that quiet face. He's told me on nights when the ouzo quiets her he can turn and gaze at her alcohol-becalmed face and almost feel a kind of love for her. He's told me once or twice, when she's gone quiet after enough ouzo, he's almost kissed her himself.

After Karl told me that, I started having dreams of being back on that stage wallowing in the filth that spilled out of the sliced-open gator with Rachel's perfect face in my hands, and then I'm sewing her head onto my left shoulder—or in some versions having someone else sew her head on my shoulder—and she is with me and I'm kissing her and the things her tongue does in my mouth are a miracle. Sometimes, though, when I dream of taking on the head of Rachel, it's not a good dream. Rachel's head, beside mine, just turns away from me, refuses me, and the pain of my longing for her, and her refusal of me, twists my body into a grotesque grimace of the human form and all I can do is a sad and stumbling two-step in some bar where the saw dust on the floor rises with my every grace-less step into clouds that could be the edges of storm fronts moving in to lay everything to waste. Dreams can leave us in places as bad as any the world can ever take us to.

Gloria's looking particularly fine, and the way that wait-ress get-up announces every curve of her ample body's almost enough to send me out to hunt snakes in the woods. But it's too dark already to have any real shot of finding the snake with my sins on it. Dark enough who knows what I might find. The other evening, when it was still much lighter than this, I stumbled over an exposed root and my hand reached out and clutched the trunk of a fir to break my fall and I felt what turned out to be words in Spanish carved into the tree. Though shallow now, when they were first carved into the tree they must have been carved deep. Only part of the sentence remained, and I only recognized a few of the Spanish words, but I had heard of the man who had long ago carved his sig-nature under that almost-gone sentence. Hernando de Soto was the name scrawled under that sentence I believe spoke of his longing for gold and his despair over how it eluded him. Too often what we ask of the world goes unanswered, though maybe the odds get better when what we desire of the world is help in repenting. Maybe the longings of the spirit are what the earth most wants to satisfy. Like to think that could be so, that in time the earth will send up the scarlet snake with my sins etched on its skin so I can be saved and made whole again. So that the ghost of a woman's perfect face will cease to haunt me.

Some nights I stay in the woods till dawn. On clear nights the stars reflect in the calm water of Lake Conasauga with such accuracy it's almost as if there's another world in this one. A better world maybe, I think on such nights. A world where a gator doesn't swallow up a woman and carry her face inside as if it were holy. Where a sister doesn't have to hunker on a stage pressing the severed hips and legs of her brother to her chest. And where a preacher doesn't have to hold in his hands, filthy with the innards of a gator, the bodiless head of a woman he loved in sin. On such nights sin almost falls away from me, and off in the distant, dimly-lit dark I imagine a naked woman humming hymns she'd played the hell out of on church organs. I picture Rachel headed in my direction, and as she gets closer the music she hums changes, grows more fervent, almost as though the music she makes with her lips and her tongue and the depths of her throat is a kind of Geiger counter, ticking more and more rapidly as she nears the man who loves her beyond all faith. It's my body she's seeking those nights, and sin has no hold on any man or woman alive in a garden with two identical skies.

One night lying beside Conasauga, listening to the muskellunge now and then leap from the lake's calm surface and fall back to the black water sending ripples through the second sky so that its moon seemed to shiver with some forbidden passion, I thought of Karl and his Greek-speaking second head and wondered which head Rachel would have kissed more if she'd ever made love to Karl. Almost asleep, I pictured Rachel moving atop Karl the way she had moved over me so many times, and then Rachel was kissing the woman's head, and the woman's head whispered something into Rachel's mouth. Asleep and dreaming, what the woman's head on Karl's left shoulder was saying was louder and more insistent and it wasn't Greek at all, ancient or modern. "Rachel," she whispered. "Love me, Rachel," she said and gently bit Rachel's lower lip. And Rachel's body and Karl's body blurred and became one body and it was Rachel's head on Karl's shoulder and the two heads were kissing and Karl's body stopped below the ribs, ending in a jaggedness of flesh and bone and someone was whimpering off in the darkness of some rotted-out stage and it was me.

Though it was hard to make him understand about the snakes, how I'd come to believe our sins are written in colors and patterns along their bodies, Karl gets how difficult it is to find the one snake with my sins inscribed on its skin. "Think of all the sinning that goes on every night and every day in this fallen world," I've told him. "If all sin is recorded on the skins of scarlet snakes, imagine the odds of coming across the one snake in all the world with your sins written across its legless body." How unlikely salvation is, Karl gets more than most.

"Faith takes each of us on a different journey," he has said to me before.

"And gives each of us different burdens," I added. Both Karl's heads, it seemed, nodded at that.

Tonight Gloria's whole body seems to lean towards the earth, and her smile is a sort of pained thing that doesn't fit her face. Makes me think that if I were to slip her uniform off I'd find bruises on her body, and the bruises would form arcane symbols on her flesh, runes that, if chanted correctly into the night air beside a lake high enough up a mountain that the moon in the sky and the moon in the lake could converse, would be both a prayer for strength and a blessing of tenderness. What I don't want to think I'd find beneath that waitress get-up is scales instead of skin, scales whose colors spell out my sins with such clarity they could never be forgiven.

Karl's Greek-speaking woman's head, quiet most of the evening, is all of a sudden ranting. "Someone must've watered down the ouzo," Karl says. As his tormentor spews what sounds like a barrage of curses in ancient Greek, Karl tells me when she's like this he gets to where he believes he could kill her. "Right now," Karl says, "I'd like to take a knife and shove it in her mouth and push it up till it pokes out the top of her skull. I'd like to skewer her," Karl says.

What stops him is what always stops him. Not being sure what killing her would mean for him. "If all it would mean," he's told me, "is that I'd have to lug a dead woman's head around with me the rest of my life, I'd do it in a minute. Hell, maybe they could even cut her off me once she's dead."

"Would they throw me in jail? Would it be murder," Karl has asked me more than once, "or would they charge me with attempted suicide?" What scares Karl the most is that killing the woman's head that drunkenly rants in Greek most nights into his left ear might be the death of him, too. "Just how much a part of me is she?" Karl has said. She's gone quiet again, and he glances at her without turning his head.

Gloria brings Karl and me another round, and another ouzo, too. Karl's drinking Stroh's and I wonder what kind of hangover he might have in the morning. Folks say mixing different types of alcohol is a prescription for a major hangover, and, since Karl and the ouzo-drinking woman's head share one body, it seems a bad idea for Karl to be downing beers.

"Karl, maybe you should drink whiskey, or vodka." Something more akin to ouzo, is my point.

"I'll be damned if I'm going to let her determine what I drink." The way he says this, it's clear how much she's already taken from him.

Sent away, is the more accurate term for it, Karl has said. "My wife and son, my siblings, almost all my friends," he said, giving me a little smile. Seems that, though he's had this woman's head on his shoulder all his life, it wasn't till she started speaking that he started losing everything that mattered to him. Karl's told me she'd been mute most of his life. "Then," Karl said, "when we were baptizing our son, right there in church she started in to speaking what turned out, according to the priest, to be ancient Greek." He said he recognized a word here and there. "No one could ignore her after that."

She was quiet the night he told me this, just a little muttering under her ouzo sweet-stinking breath. Occasionally what I'd call a whimper. "Can't even work no more," Karl said. Said his boss told him that since she started talking, having him around made everyone else in the shop nervous. "Disability pay's what I live on now. Only one hooker will even deign to service me," Karl said, "and she makes me pay double." I laughed at that but stopped when I saw the look on Karl's face. Hell, even his tormentor's face gave me a look that told me how offended she was. She muttered something in that arcane Greek of hers and swallowed more ouzo.

"Miracles do happen, Karl." I mean to offer him some semblance of hope that he might one day be free of his foreign tormentor, but Karl takes what I say differently.

"You might call this a miracle," he says with a nod to the left of his head, "but she ain't no miracle. This here's a damnation, is what she is. Some sort of demon," Karl says. "Not even hell wanted her so I got stuck with her. I gave up long ago trying to figure out what sin I'd committed," Karl says, "to justify this. Must have been so awful I've blocked it out. Repressed the memory of whatever I did to earn this vexation, is what I've done," Karl says. "If you come across a snake out in the woods having trouble crawling for the weight of the sins inscribed in its scales," he says, "that's the one with *my* sins on it."

Karl not only knows of my searching, he knows I used to be a preacher and that I worked with faith healers back in the day. "Too bad that gator ate that boy healer," he said once. "Sounds like maybe he could have freed me of her. Maybe he could have spoken to her in what used to be called tongues and convinced her to go back to hell. Don't know if that Phineas could have helped me none, though," Karl said. "Hell, I'd be afraid what might happen if she were to swallow one of his worms." I didn't bother to remind him it was Phineas who swallowed the worms, not those in need of healing.

Phineas and the boy and all the rest are gone now, so it's not like it mattered he was confused as to what they did. None of them are doing anything no more. And all I'm doing is trying to find a snake with my sins on it to cut up and fry with some onions and peppers so I can eat it and be set free from the ghost of a woman's face that haunts me every bit as much as Karl's second head haunts him, that head humming something that sounds very old and very sad in Karl's left ear.

Humming don't seem to work for me like it worked for Jebediah. Every afternoon I head out into one of the pine forests. Some I can hike to and others I have to drive to, they're so far off. The Chattahoochee National Park covers some ground. I make sure the sun is almost ready to drop down out of sight before I start in to humming, and the tune I hum is the closest I can recall to what Jebediah used to hum when he was out gathering snakes. Jebediah's music brought snakes out of the earth every time. Must be I have the tune wrong. My ear for music was never all that exact, though when Rachel played a church organ I'd swear every note echoed in my body for days.

Gloria's humming as she brings Karl and his tormentor and me another round. It's no hymn she's humming.

"What's that tune?" Karl says. His tormentor has started whistling what Gloria's humming.

"What? Was I humming?" Gloria says and smiles, and goes back to her humming with a look on her face like she's listening to herself to try to name that tune. Not one of us can say what tune it is but it's catchy, that's for sure. Not only is Karl's tormentor whistling it in his left ear, Karl and I start in to humming it too. Pretty soon all four of us are going at it like it's some symphony we're performing, each of us taking a different pitch.

Several of the other Marlow's regulars join in and soon just about everyone drinking in this dive is humming this tune not one of us can name. Jimmy over at the bar is using his unwashed beer glasses as percussion, and Gloria is dancing with the music we're all making, this music she started without knowing she was humming. Seems everyone in this bar was waiting for something to call them out of themselves, to get them to celebrate just being here and having had enough to drink to make a song no one recognizes infectious enough to pull us all into it. Karl just kissed his tormentor. It's all something to see.

I want to remember this tune and take it with me into the woods. Maybe this is the music that will bring out my snake and let me kiss the ghost of Rachel's face a last time before letting it go. Gloria's looking at me with her arms out. In the uncertain light of this place, she looks enough like forgiveness to get me up and moving in front of all these humming fools in this place of faith they call Subligna. Could be I've still got some dancing left in me.

TO GIVE GHOSTS THE FINGER

You're not going to believe this story. Hell, even I don't believe it, and I'm its only teller now. Sitting in that dim cell across from Jebediah, though, listening to him tell it, there was no question. I believed it. While Jebediah told it. The minute I left that cell and looked back to see him on the edge of his bunk, eyes closed and something, almost a smile, his mouth was doing, all closed off and gone silent, I wondered if I'd been had. But I didn't doubt that, were I to listen to him tell the story again, I'd believe it so long as he was telling it. Some things just don't make sense. It's just how they are.

Leaving that cell, what was on my mind was if there was a way to get the jury to render an immediate decision after listening to Jebediah testify. Though, as it turned out, I didn't have to worry about the jury.

I was warned, before I went in to see him, that Jebediah had once been a healer who worked with snakes. You don't hear about many folks like Jebediah any more. The days of the traveling ministries with their tag teams of preachers and healers are all but over, a kind of colorful history the locals chew the fat over. Least ways, that's my impression of things. Course, I'm an educated man. Hell, I don't even go to church regularly, something Mary Jo is on my case about these days. So the guards and their stories didn't much affect me.

If he starts up that humming of his, one guard told me, watch out. I've heard it said that if the humming gets in you,

you might do anything and not remember. Hell, you might end up in here yourself, lawyer, for something you don't have no recollection of doing.

The gullibility of some folks is just amazing, I thought. But that was before I heard Jebediah's story. This story I can't say I believe but keep on telling as if it's the God's honest truth.

As if a lawyer could recognize such a thing, is no doubt what you're thinking. I don't blame you for thinking that. But I wasn't born a lawyer, no sir. My momma made sure I was raised in the fear of God. Took me to church every Sunday and made me sit without squirming in those hard pews while the preacher told us all what sinners we were and how it was only through Christ we could be saved. Growing up I believed, without a doubt. Now, doubt is all I'm left with to try to make sense of this world some folks say has turned its back on God.

I say the world can't turn its back on God, but God, well, he could turn his back on us. And often it seems that's just what he's done. There are times I just have to believe that, or nothing makes sense at all.

I didn't ask for Jebediah's case, you know. I'm a public defender. I was appointed to represent him. Jebediah had been charged with the murder of his wife. It was said he killed her and then dumped her body in the swamp for the gators to take care of. The prosecutor had witnesses, including a broken-down preacher, who all claimed to have been at a healing when a gator was cut open and the remains of Jebediah's wife spilled out. I never got a chance to see all the forensic evidence the prosecutor had gotten from the remains, so I don't know how good a case they could have presented, or what effect that evidence might have had on my belief in Jebediah's story.

As he was telling it at least. I could ask to see the evidence now, but now I don't want to see it. I want the story, not the truth, and I'm afraid I can't have both.

Mary Jo says she's worried about me. The other night we were in bed and damp, our breath still a bit ragged but calming down. My finger was teasing her, down there where she was all juices and heat. Mary Jo reached down and ran her finger over my thing and it jumped a little and she grabbed it. So there she was, holding me like that, with my finger twirling around and making her give out little gasps now and again, and she lets out with how she's worried about me.

Ever since that client of yours hanged himself in his cell, you haven't exactly been yourself, Mary Jo said, and gave a little squeeze.

Why, whatever do you mean, my lady, I said, and slipped my finger inside her. Just who am I if I'm not your husband, and what in heaven's name are you doing with whoever's finger this is inside you like this? We both laughed at that, and I started moving my finger around inside her. She forgot about my not being myself.

But she's right. Whoever I was before the day I walked into Jebediah's cell, I'm not that man any more. The story is what has made me someone else. This story I can't even say I believe but feel compelled to tell.

Wish I could tell it how Jebediah told it in that jail cell. But then, his conviction in telling it came from his having lived it. Having lived it trumps absurdity every time. Faith can't overcome what is too absurd to believe, but living it is another matter. Living it, and having to live with it, is something none of us can deny. No matter how much we may want to.

The guard tells me you used to heal people with snakes, I said to Jebediah after the guard brought me in and told him I was his court-appointed attorney.

Jebediah looked me over and smiled. No sir, he said. Healing only folks who had snakes would have been a rather limited practice, don't you think?

I could tell he wanted to chuckle at that, but he played it straight. He was testing me, I knew. To see how smart I was, how quick. I was impressed with Jebediah right off.

Now that depends, I said.

On what?

On what you mean by saying people with snakes. I mean, that could include not only folks who kept snakes as pets, which I'd have to agree would make up a probably quite small portion of the population of any town. But if it also includes folks whose homes have been infested with snakes, or even a single snake, living either in the walls of their dining room, say, or under the house in what most folks call the crawl space, then the number goes up considerably. And if you then add people whose children wake up screaming regularly from having dreams of snakes being in their bed or under it, well now it's getting to be a rather respectable number. And if you add to that the number of plumbers in town, well now you've certainly got enough folks who might be in need of healing that you could make quite a good living.

Jebediah smiled and nodded. A fly lifted off his head with the nod and buzzed around his face till he feebly swatted at it with a rather large hand and dazed it enough that it had to land on his bunk where it shook itself before flying out through the iron bars and towards the window. You'll do, he said.

I like to get right down to it with a client. So, did you do it? I said.

Well, sir, he started, that's really a question of responsibility, ain't it? Now, the answer might depend on just how far you want to stretch that question, how far from the actual act responsibility reaches.

Like I said, he impressed me right off. Jebediah was no dummy.

Fair enough, I said. Without any sense of what was to come, I told Jebediah, Why don't you just tell me your story. And that's what he did.

Like they told you, sir, he said, I used to heal people. I traveled all around back in the day with a preacher and some singers. We'd set up tents at the edge of a town and put up posters all over, brightly-colored posters so as to get folk's attention. The posters, they'd proclaim, in big letters, a faith-healing had come to town, and they'd include the time and the place when the healing would commence.

Even before the posters went up, Jebediah said, I'd have gone out into whatever fields or forests I found near where our tents flapped in what wind there was and, with my old canvas sack in my hand, I'd start to humming.

Humming? I said, looking up from my note pad.

Yes, sir, humming. No doubt the guard warned you about that, he said.

I nodded. Go on, I said.

There I'd be, out in some field or among some trees, with my sack, humming. I can't tell you, sir, why it was snakes came out to my humming. All I know is that whenever I went looking for snakes for the show and started in to humming, the snakes came up out of their holes in the ground and let me pick them up and place them in the sack. You need to understand, sir, these was harmless snakes, mostly garter snakes or rat snakes. Never any snake that was poisonous. The humming just brought out the harmless ones. Don't know why, sir. Just the way it was.

Rachel never did care for the snakes, he said, though she never told me why.

Rachel, I said. That was your wife's name?

She was my wife. Yes, sir. Though I can't say now that I ever really knew who she was when she was with me. We was married more than three years, and not once did I ever touch her, sir. You know, in a sexual way. I thought she was too good for that sort of sweating and such, sir. Turned out I couldn't have been more wrong. But back then, I believed things more easily than I do now.

So, during the healing them snakes would become vessels to hold the sins of the folks I was healing and would turn poisonous with them sins, and I'd have to snap their necks soon as they'd absorbed all the sin there was in a person. After a show, I'd dump the dead snakes in some ditch and forget about them. They was just snakes, after all, sir. Just instruments to be used in the name of the Lord.

Rachel and me done this healing gig a few years together. She'd play the organ for the singers and as a kind of background for the healings, too. She could bring a music out of any old organ that was just as sweet as heaven itself must be. Proof of her goodness, I thought, of her purity. Now I know music comes from something other than purity.

Was your wife unfaithful? I said.

Can't say as I can answer that question, sir. I never thought she was, but I was blinded back then, I guess. Blinded by my love for her, or who I believed she was. It was the finger, sir, that pointed out who she really was, I guess you could say.

The finger? I said. What finger? The flies seemed to be congregating in Jebediah's cell, almost as if to hear the story. I had to keep swatting them off my pad.

I don't remember what town it was in, but I heard these rumors of what was said to be a holy relic. Rumor was this relic had been stolen from the Vatican, that the Pope had issued some kind of decree or whatnot demanding its return. Word was there were folks all over the world looking for the relic, and all the time it was in a broken-down shack in this godforsaken backwater of a town I can't even recall the name of.

The relic, it was said, sir, was the middle finger of Christ's right hand. The story was that some Roman guard had hacked the finger off while Christ was still on the cross, but after he'd died. The guard, it's said, wanted a souvenir. It's said he'd done this with others, that he had many such fingers. But this finger, so the story goes, was different. This finger didn't rot. To this day, the rumor was, the finger was perfectly preserved. Could have just been cut off a person's hand, they said.

I know what you're thinking, sir. Why don't the Bible mention the missing middle finger of Christ? The way I heard it, the apostles felt it would ruin the story of the resurrection. They couldn't have the body ascending to heaven minus a finger. And they certainly couldn't have the risen Christ, before he ascends to sit with his father, going around in search of the finger. It just wouldn't have been dignified, they decided, and so they left it out of the gospels.

Someone told me though, sir, there are other holy texts not included in the Bible, for whatever reasons. And they say the missing finger of Christ is recorded in one of those other texts. Don't know if it's true or not, sir. I've never read those other texts. But I had heard tell of them before. So I believed it could be true, the story of the Roman guard cutting off the finger of Christ.

And once I believed the story, I wanted that finger, sir, became obsessed with having to have it. The power that must still be in that finger, I thought, even after a couple of thousand years. It was too much of a temptation for me. And, it turned out, for Rachel, too. Had I been able to foresee what would happen with the finger, sir, I would have given up searching for it and left that town without finding it. But I was just a healer, sir. Never had the gift of prophecy.

I let the preacher head off for the next town without me, told him I had some personal business I needed to tend to. Told him Rachel would go on with him and the rest, that I'd join them in a few days at most. I didn't tell the preacher nothing about the rumor of Christ's finger. I wanted it for myself.

It took more than a week to track that finger down. By the time I found the man who had it, hidden away under some loose floor boards in his shack, I was so filled with my need to possess the finger that an eloquence I'd never had before had come upon me and so I was able to convince that poor man that it was God's will the finger come into my hands. I moved him so with my words that he gladly pulled the floor boards up himself and wrapped the finger in a silk handkerchief that had belonged to his late wife before handing it to me with his blessing.

How that old man had come to be keeper of Christ's finger is something I can't rightly say, as I never thought to ask the question. History was something I couldn't have cared less about, sir, back then. It was all about getting the finger.

When I caught up with the preacher and Rachel and the others, I got Rachel off alone and showed her the finger and told her whose finger it was. She gazed at that perfectly-preserved large middle finger, larger even than mine and I was always told I have large hands, and something came over her face. I thought, sir, it was what the preacher would have called a look of beatitude, a kind of holy respect for the finger because of whose finger it was. I didn't recognize lust on Rachel's face. I'd never seen it there before.

After storing the finger safely away in our things, I headed off to gather the snakes and then went into town with some of the others to put up posters, believing the finger would be safe where I had hidden it. After all, no one but Rachel even knew of the finger, so no one, I thought, would be looking for it.

I have to admit, sir, that by this time my motives were not completely pure. Sure, I had thought about the possible healing power of the finger. But if I used it for healing, what Christ had done with it of course, everyone would find out about the finger and would want to get their hands on it. So I had started to think of other ways to use the power of the finger. To look for oil, for example. Surely the finger could point to where I'd find millions of barrels of oil. Or surely the cut off finger of our Lord could point to which horse was going to win a race. Surely that would not be beyond the power of our Lord and savior's finger, is what I thought.

All thinking stopped, sir, when I came back to our tent after collecting the snakes and putting up posters. Rachel was on the bed and moaning in a way I had never heard. I thought she was sick and ran over to ask what was the matter when I saw it. Rachel, my wife, who I had thought so pure I had never touched her, had that finger in her delicate hand and was plunging it into her parts down there. The finger was making a soft sucking sound as she pushed it into herself and pulled it out to the fingernail before pushing it all the way back in while she kept on moaning in what I understood was rapture rather than pain. She was so full of that finger, and what it was doing to her, she didn't even know I was there until I reached down as the finger was nearly out of her and grabbed it from her.

She half opened her eyes. I don't know if she even knew who I was. Maybe she thought I was Jesus himself, come back to join together with his lost finger. Please, she said. Please.

I turned away from her, sir, moaning and writhing in our bed, her small hands reaching out to me for the finger, and walked out of that tent and kept walking till I came to a swamp where I hurled that accursed finger as far as I could. I heard it hit the water, and then I just kept on walking, away from Rachel and the preacher and that life of healing. None of it was for me no more, sir. That much I was sure of.

I can't say, sir, how Rachel ended up in that gator. Though I believe she followed the finger of Christ. Maybe she could smell herself on the finger and followed that smell right on into the swamp. I just kept walking, sir, till they grabbed me and put handcuffs on me and told me they was arresting me for killing my wife.

It's that question of responsibility, sir, like I said before. I mean, I did find the finger of our Lord and I did tell Rachel about it and I did rip it out of her and hurl it into that swamp, which is what led her to the swamp and the gator that swallowed her, I reckon. Maybe that is enough to make me guilty, sir. And maybe it's more that means I'm guilty. After all, it was me not touching her all those nights. Maybe had I been touching her, like a husband should touch his wife, maybe Rachel could have resisted the temptation of the savior's finger.

I looked up from my notes then, and what I saw still haunts me. I saw a man who could not forgive himself his life. There was this look about him that was more powerful than anything I've ever seen in any jail cell. Yes, I was moved by his guilt, by how his guilt had broken him into something he would not have said, I'm sure, was Jebediah.

I told him I believed we had a good case, and that I would start looking for witnesses who could corroborate his story. He looked at me like he wanted to laugh, but just nodded his head.

The next day the guard told me he had hung himself from the pipe just under the ceiling in his cell. The guard said he used his clothes, tied together. He was found this morning, sir, the guard said, swinging naked from the pipe, smiling, dead.

Mary Jo says maybe going to church will help. I want to believe she could be right. I want to believe I can stop telling this story, stop being haunted by Jebediah. And by Rachel. And that finger. Maybe church is just where I need to go. Maybe I'll ask for sanctuary. If the church can grant me sanctuary, maybe I can finally give all the ghosts the finger, and mean it.

FISHING THE SKY WITHOUT BAIT

Daddy John attracts UFOs. Folks say nobody knows why he does, and truth is nobody wants him to stop. Fact is, folks encourage him to keep it up. The lights, they say, is so pretty at night. The young uns like the lights.

When I was a young un myself, my Uncle Sid used to sit for me nights my ma had to work. Uncle Sid was a talker, despite his stutter, and would tell me all kinds of what he liked to call epic stories that involved him and his buddies drinking too much and getting into trouble. Uncle Sid was still a drinker and more than once, after he'd had half a bottle or so of the whiskey he snuck in without the knowledge of my ma, who hated liquor and wouldn't truck with no one who partook of it, as she liked to say, Uncle Sid would tell me the story of Daddy John's conception. Conception was the word he used, and the first time he told me the story he had to explain what that meant. I was the most popular kid in first grade for weeks after that. Knowledge, as they say, is power.

Uncle Sid would swear he was the only one who knew how it happened, cause he was there with Daddy John's ma, my Aunt Sarah—who's not really my aunt—the night Daddy John was conceived. Uncle Sid made me swear never to tell Uncle Jackson—who's not really my uncle—the story he was about to tell me. He made me swear that every time he was drunk enough to tell me the story. Uncle Sid would say that he and

Daddy John's ma had had a thing, before Uncle Jackson and her got together, and that they'd been coming back to town after what he called a little quality time together when Daddy John had been conceived. Uncle Sid said the conception was miraculous. Biblical, he said. Said it was a dead man hanging by the side of the road, a man who, when he'd been alive, had been the brother of a faith healer, who was Daddy John's real father. Said he was witness to Daddy John's ma convincing that corpse to make her in the family way. By this time the whiskey would be making Uncle Sid more and more sleepy. He'd be mumbling bout what a miracle it was, how he'd never seen the likes of it before nor since. He'd end up mumbling "Sarah" in a voice that, even at six, was enough to make me want to start in to bawling.

I ain't never said nothing about this to Uncle Jackson or Aunt Sarah. Uncle Sid's told me that, were I to say something to either of them, Daddy John's real daddy would rise outta his grave, call his faith healer brother outta his, and the two of them would set to scaring them UFOs out of the sky to crash into the swamps around town and get sucked down under the mudded water never to be heard from again. And then, Uncle Sid told me, that dead faith healer and his brother, Daddy John's real daddy, would come and grab Daddy John outta his sleep and haul him with them back into the ground and all that would be left of Daddy John would be a little dust left dancing in the sun lighting up his empty bedroom.

I'm not saying I'm sure I believe Uncle Sid, but I'm not ready to put it to the test neither. Daddy John and me, we both have seen some things, and I guess I've seen enough to make me think the story Uncle Sid told me more than once when I was young could be true. There's something, after all, that ain't quite right about Daddy John. And the UFOs, they're just the latest incarnation. Incarnation. That's a word I learned in church, not from Uncle Sid. Heck, I doubt Uncle Sid knows the word, what it means. And I'm darn sure it would take him a while to get it said. As long or longer than it took him to stammer out conception, I'm sure.

Daddy John, who can say anything with nary a single stutter, has gotten popular. All the TV shows want him, and they promise big bucks will be his if UFOs show up with him. Dan Rather himself come to town to beg Daddy John to come on to CBS and bring his friends in the sky along.

Nobody doubts Daddy John could bring any old UFO he wanted and hold that cash in his hand. Folks say Daddy John can shout birds out of the sky and fish the local lakes without bait and catch trout.

Daddy John, he just says everything's a kind of fishing.

Daddy John, he says you just got to wait and hold to your faith, and UFOs will show up.

But Daddy John won't go on them TV shows. Says what good would all that cash do him. Says it's all about faith and what you can do with what God hangs on your back.

Daddy John says you got to know what you can catch and what you can't. If you do, he says, things'll catch you.

HYMN OF ASH

It was a tale only a fool or a saint would put much faith in. My mother put me to bed most of my childhood with the story of her healer-brother who was cut in two, his little torso and arms and head—still mouthing the rhythms of some lost prayer—swallowed by a gator on a stage where she rocked a kind of grief with his ragged hips and twitching legs in her damp arms. Such stories must be buried in every family. In most, they're just stories, and everyone who tells them feels free to shape the story to their liking and to their own particular ends. This story my mother never told different. To do so, she once tried to explain when I was grown, about to leave her house, would have been to deny what the story was, a kind of icon embedded in the brief and otherwise unremarkable history of our family.

Problem is, I'll never be confused for a saint. And I've tried my best, friend, to distance myself from the other label. Still, out of respect I suppose, I've never let myself retell the story in any words but those I can only hear in the now gone voice of my mother.

Alexander, she'd whisper, the light from the hall a dim reflection off her face and shoulders as she settled on the edge of my bed and her shadow eclipsed me. She could have been the moon, the way she glowed looming over me those nights, or some ancient goddess of alabaster marble warmed to life.

Alexander, you remember. How that picture of your uncle could set me to crying, back before I took it down off the dining room wall. And how for weeks after I'd stored it away under them fancy dinner placemats, you heard me wake up crying in the night down the hall. It was his hips, and the ragged and foul-tasting air that hovered where his stomach and chest and arms and head had been, his ripped off and sagging hips that come to me them nights, clicking a music that started my own flesh shivering under the layers of blankets I'd piled up, and started me swearing at the Lord bout his Mysterious Ways.

And then, like it was sure to lull me to sleep, she'd start in about the night before her brother's angelic face was taken into the ridged belly of the beast. The night a preacher wallowed in the spilled guts of the last gator to give itself up to the Lord through the ministrations of her brother, my uncle, who I've only seen in polaroids mailed to my mother in her grieving from the faithful, one of which she'd stuck in a gilded frame and nailed to the dining room wall for a time. The uncle I've only met in the story my mother told of him, night after night, till my childhood had become a landscape where gators crossed themselves and offered their lizard bodies up in the rigid and unforgiven shape of Jesus' rood. Till the swamp became an altar I laid myself down on in dreams my mother wanted to believe were visions. Or visitations. Her brother come back to her, out of the belly of that long since corpse of a gator. Come out of one swamp and come crawling across the cross-haunted swamp of a boy's imagining, through gator-infested nightmares, back into her arms.

It was a time of visitations, she liked to say. *A time of visitations and miracles.*

Other versions of that time have come to me in other voices since those nights of my childhood. Voices of doubt, of uncertainty. Voices that tell of a preacher gone mad amid the entrails of a gator, rapt, held in what was left of the arms of an organist. Voices that speak of sin and failure and a world of bodies lost and wandering and looking. Always, the bodies summoned by these voices are off in search of something lost or missing. Always, this wandering and this lostness is, the voices say, emblematic of how we are lost in our own flesh. It's a lesson, these voices say, a parable, like those Jesus himself used. And like those parables, the real story is left for us to discover, each of us alone with our private fears and doubts and lusts.

It was a code, they'd say. A code to keep the damned from finding the path to salvation. Only those with the key, the very heart of Jesus I've seen painted red and glowing, on fire in his opened chest, could find heaven, that fiery heart itself the key. Without that heart, the damned were doomed. Only one path to salvation, they'd say.

Has this ever bothered you, friend? I mean, aren't we told Jesus walked and sailed and walked some more, when he wasn't riding on the back of some worn-out donkey, preaching and healing and changing the world? How do I reconcile this Jesus with the one who spoke in code, so that only the *right* people were saved? Wasn't the whole point he came down to suffer among us to save us, *all* of us, not just those who already knew the way? How, friend, are we supposed to reconcile the various Jesuses that have come down to us out of a past never as holy as some would have us believe? And how am I to rid myself, ever, of this radiant spectre whispering, even now, through my sleep, her story, grotesque as it is, of a conflict between a weary god and a devil that doesn't ever tire?

My mother did tire, though, at the end. At the end there was no doubt. She'd had enough of this world and its heart-aches. Even her skin was tired, the way it refused light, seemed to reject it out of hand, as she lay back in her sick bed and struggled to breathe. At her request, the drapes were left closed, the only light in the room coming from the few candles kept burning beside the bed, burning for their scents as much as for any light they put out. Isn't that how saints die, a kind of willed and gradual fading from this world into the next? Sometimes, I like to think my mother could have been a saint. Not one of the named ones. Not one of the proper Roman Catholic ones old women pray to with beads of wood rubbed smooth by their rough fingers. My mother, if she was any kind of saint, was the sort that did her work anonymous. It's the anonymous saints, though, that do the hard work, the true work of whatever there is left of God in this world. Of that I'm as sure as I am of anything.

Hiddenness, that's the nature of things these days. As if the whole damned world is some cursed parable, meaning lying somewhere just to the left or the right of wherever it is we are, or think we are. My mother, who had seen more than her share of demons and angels, enough to sometimes confuse them in memory, one for the other, she used to swear God himself sometimes lost track of things. *There's just too much, anymore, in this world,* she'd say. *No room, anymore,* she'd sigh, *for something as fragile as prayer.* She'd stopped praying, she told me, after the night she held the hips and twitching legs of her brother in her arms. The night that gator, lazy, its belly full of torso and arms, the small hands clasped in prayer, waltzed out of that tent and back to the swamp. Some voices lead us astray, of that I'm sure, and sometimes it's hard to know which voice is true, authentic is the word I've heard used, and which is the voice of a demon disguised. So much hiddenness in the world anymore, it's hard to tell.

Like you, now, friend, questioning this story that haunts me, my family heritage, this parable of hunger and forgiveness. If you'd been there and listened to my mother tell the story her last night in this world, in the exact words she'd told it all those nights when I was a child, despite the raspy struggle of her breathing, nothing left out, if you'd been there in that dim room where shadows twitched, it seemed, with her strained breaths, you wouldn't be so quick to say it's just a story. Fiction has a certain feel to it. If you'd been there that night you'd know this story she told had nothing of the feel of fiction about it. If you'd been there and leaned over her now and then to dry the spittle from the corners of her withered mouth, you wouldn't sit there smug, sipping lukewarm beer and shaking your head, trying to tell me stories just get in the way, that I need to let it go, to stop telling the story.

My mother may have stopped praying, but she never doubted God was alive and thinking over the world. Faith was a thing she said none of us can do without, not if we're going to ever feel at ease in this life. We can kill off everything else, she'd say, but we can't kill off faith, or our need to have it in our hearts as we stumble from the past to the future. My mother's voice is a live and twitching thing inside me still.

My own story, friend, is, as my mother would call it, a story of visitations. Not those dreamed arrivals of half her brother, the half the gator waltzed off with, but the visits of other figures, like the tall, smoking figure I thought was no more family than in that vague manner in which we can all be said to be family. A stranger, I thought, when he knocked on my door.

After my mother's death, I went through a period of violence bred by an anger I couldn't name. Finally, I packed what little I thought of as my own and, remembering summers spent in the cabin my mother's father built, disappeared into the woods in search of it, as if it could offer me some peace I couldn't find anywhere else. It was falling in on itself when I came to it, and my first months there were spent in hard labor, healing the damage the years and weather had done. Beams needed shoring up with the trunks of young trees I felled with the axe I found in the cabin, and holes in the roof needed patching with shingles I had to buy in the small town a few miles to the north.

Not much of a town. A gas station, hardware store, a church, a train station and warehouse, a bar, what passed for a grocery store, a hair salon, and a few houses lined up along cross streets that petered out after a few blocks, ending in fields of corn or soy or in woods, depending on the direction. It was enough for my needs, though I never saw the inside of the church in that town. I guess, for some time after the death of my mother, I had no use for God or any of his trappings here in this world.

The inside of the bar was another thing. After days of nothing but work I'd take a break and spend a few hours with nearly voiceless men drinking whiskey and beer in Billy's. That was the name on the window of the bar. Billy's. One thing more than anything else about that bar stays with me. The painting over the mirror. Most bars I've spent time in over the years, if there's any artwork behind the bar, it's of vast, open landscapes, like that one there, or if not open land then some kind of wild creatures, deer and bear being most prevalent. Not Billy's. In Billy's what you saw if you looked up was a dark canvas, almost as if the painting itself was charred, of a house being engulfed in flames. Night, clouded-over, moonless, surrounded the burning house, flames offering the only light.

Despite the years between me and the nights I spent drinking myself sick in that desolate place, that painting's still clear in my memory. I remember animals, dogs perhaps, or maybe something larger, maybe deer, moving off into the dark, the flicker of shadows all they were anymore, but there. Of that I would swear. Just as I'm sure I remember the two figures still in the house, bending to the burning of the flesh off their bones. A man and a woman, of that I have no doubt, both on fire and visible in the frame of what must have been a picture window before the house was nothing but flames. Sometimes, after a night of alcohol and staring at that painting, everything and everyone in that bar was covered in soot and smoldering, as if the world was nothing but ash and a few dying embers. Delusion, sometimes, is all we're left with to believe in.

I believe in the burned-out shell of that bar. I believe in the ash that settled on the charred bodies of men who were voiceless, their tongues faint memories of ash down their throats. I believe in the gasps of smoke when they opened their mouths the way they remembered opening them to speak, back before the flames had taken all they had to say. I believe in the sad music someone kept slipping blackened quarters into the juke box to listen to over and over, slow-dancing with the smoke. Nothing, I believe, had escaped the fire. Warm beers up and down the bar sweated and left circles of faded ash.

My visitor, it could be he'd been in that bar, maybe even in the burning house that turned it into a place of ash and sorrow. His body was smoking when he knocked on the cabin's door. At first I didn't realize he'd brought the smoke with him, that it was, in fact, him smoking. This dark figure leaned against the frame of the door surrounded by ragged wisps of smoke I took to be fog. It was, after all, dusk, the time for fog. But there was no fog anywhere past the dark and voiceless figure propped up against my door. Had he been delivered there by someone who had knocked for him and then run off?

Whoever or whatever had brought him to my door, it was clear he wasn't going anywhere soon. Not without help. I'm not sure how, exactly, my arm came to be around him and supporting him as I led him in, but once that arm was his support, any question about what the poor soul had been through dissolved in the suddenly sooty air around the two of us hunkering our way towards the couch. Ash covered every inch of clothing he wore, the exposed flesh of his arms and neck and face smudged with an oily grime that came off on my hands and clothes as I walked him over the bare wood floor and lowered him onto the couch.

Which is where he remained for days, in what was a sleep that might have been a coma. Though he'd been barely conscious when I found him leaning against the cabin, and seemed vaguely aware I was another person on whom he was leaning, by the time his body and its private trauma was settled on the couch it could not be said he was aware of the couch, the cabin, me, or even his own body, shattered and shuddering as it was.

At times his body remained utterly still, and I would have to bend down close and place my ear to his lips to be sure he was still breathing. Other times, his body shook so violently I had to pick him up off the floor and heave him back onto the couch, the air around him, on those occasions, almost an aura, thickened with the shivering loose of the soot that covered him. Whatever he had been through, fire was a part of it, that much was certain.

Though fire wasn't the whole of it. On the second day of his odd, febrile coma, not able to wake him and not able to stomach the ash that had started to collect everywhere in the cabin, spread by his breath and his occasional attacks of feverish, futile motion, armed with a sponge, a bucket of warm water, and a bar of soap, I worked over his exposed flesh, trying to remove what seemed a kind of tar that did not want to let go of his flesh, like it had bonded with it. It took almost the entire morning, but by the early part of the afternoon my visitor was looking almost human, breathing so quiet he might have been dead. That afternoon, whispering apologies to his unconscious body, I stripped him of the blackened clothes he wore. The clouds of ash that hovered around us, had they been in the sky and looking like they did in the air of the cabin, would have terrified every animal in the woods. Those clouds hung in a line from the couch to the door of the cabin the rest of the day. It wasn't till the next morning I was able to use the small vacuum I'd bought in town to take up the ash from where it had settled on the floor and the meager furniture.

After stripping him, armed with a new bucket of warm water, the sponge, and what was left of the soap, I washed the body that had been hidden under the clothes, a lean and solid body, and found the tattoo on his left thigh of a trapeze, marking this body, I thought, passing the sponge over it, as the body of an acrobat, a body meant to fly through the air, to take the breath of the crowd below and use it to stay aloft longer than would have seemed humanly possible. But it was clear this body knew of the ground, too. Huge, blotchy bruises covered most of the torso, front and back, bruises that, read right, might be a map of whatever world this acrobat had escaped from. Smaller but just as ghastly bruises streaked his lean but muscular legs. Not even his arms had gotten out unscathed, with small bruises, the size of fists, I thought, along both upper arms and the forearms marked with gashes, as if some demon from hell had slashed at him through the fire enveloping his body. Maybe the demon had tried to grab hold of the acrobat, to pull him down into the fiery air of hell itself to perform his art for the hordes of the damned. Whatever it was this man had been through, I thought, he would not be speaking of it for a very long time, even if he did, finally, wake up. He would wake without language, of that I was sure.

And so he did. It was on the third day. I was treating the wounds on his forearms with what was left of the alcohol and iodine from the cabinet in the bathroom. At first, it seemed one of his attacks was starting, and I backed off to wait it out. But I set the bottle down when I realized his breathing had changed. He was almost snoring. Without putting my ear up to his lips, I could distinctly hear the intake and release of his breathing, which seemed a good sign, like he was getting stronger. When he opened his eyes I was standing over him smiling, most of the evidence of whatever hell he'd been through gone. The subtle muscles of his face were apparently not yet healed. The slash of his mouth across his face formed a distorted grimace that unnerved me, friend.

How do you feel? I whispered, thinking that after at least three days of silence a whisper was what was called for. It did not yet seem time for the normal tones of a human voice.

His mouth opened, letting go an inarticulate rasp, along with a breath-cloud of ash. His body shook with the force of a cough and bent into a fetal position. After several more coughs, several more clouds of ash, his aerial form still hunched up into a position fit for the womb, his eyes closed and his breathing made it clear he was asleep again, exhausted from his feeble attempt to communicate. I replaced the thin blanket covering his naked body and left him to sleep. When he was ready, he would try again to speak, though it would yet be days before the first recognizable word flew through those lips. And that would be a name, the name of a man I had never known, though I'd been told he was some relation.

The next day, a little after noon, his eyes opened for the second time. Just minutes before, I had finished cleaning up after his body, its necessary functions. I was in the kitchen and didn't know he was awake until I heard what sounded like some animal stepping cautiously into the cabin and turned to find him standing there, naked, trembling as he took in his surroundings. His eyes jerked around until they focused on a black and white photograph my grandfather had told me was of some distant relative of mine. He never told me more than that, always saying I had to ask my mother about it. My mother died without ever making good on her promise to tell me, some day, just who it was in that picture.

The man in the grainy photograph was stripped to the waist. There was some kind of bright, focused light centered on his chest. His sweaty, muscular torso gleamed. His right arm was raised up over his head, which was tilted back, the mouth open, as if to swallow the fist. Held tight in that fist, but blurred with motion the way the camera will do, was what looked like some huge worm. If it was a worm, which my grandfather swore it was, it was a worm like no worm I'd ever seen. To this day, friend, believe it or not, I have yet to see a worm like the worm forever about to be swallowed by that huge man in that black and white photograph.

My visitor's legs, despite their musculature, trembled under him, his arms crossed at his chest until he moved one to point at the photograph of the man about to swallow an unearthly worm, and his mouth opened. No sound came, but a little cloud of ash drifted down over his body, catching in the thick curly hairs that covered his chest and groin.

I don't know who that is, I said, more than a whisper but not loud enough, I hoped, to shock my visitor back into his ashen torpor. He turned from the photograph to me, his mouth opening, again without sound, just the slight drift down of ash over his body. What if, I worried, his voice never returned? I started to imagine his tongue had been burned out of his mouth by whatever fire he had passed through.

You must be hungry, I said, to which he nodded, the first actual sign he understood human speech. I helped his trembling body to the table and into one of the chairs. I made him eggs and toast and brewed up another pot of coffee. He ate in silence, though every now and then I'd catch him watching me at the sink, where I was washing the pots and pans, waiting to wash his plate and silverware. Once he coughed, and later, after he was back on the couch and asleep again, but breathing normal, I cleaned the path of ash his cough had sprayed across the table. It seemed as though whatever fire he had come through was not done inside him but burned on.

A fire inside a man, imagine that. And no metaphor, either. Not the petty burning lovers like to claim for themselves, for their hearts, but a roaring, destructive blaze spreading from organ to organ. Fire still raged in my mysterious visitor. A fire filling every cavity of his body with ash. There *are* things any one of us might have to cope with that could set us to burning the way my visitor was still being burned, even as he slept almost peaceful on my couch.

The next morning I came out of the bedroom to find him standing in front of the photograph of the worm-swallower and touched his shoulder, thinking to ask what he'd like for breakfast. He turned to me, his arm raising to point a finger at the photograph. His mouth opened, he swallowed, almost as if swallowing ash so sound could make it past his lips, and, with the slightest cloud of ash, he uttered the first articulate sound he had made since I took him in and started to tend to him.

Phineas, he rasped. It was as if the sound of his own voice was a pain he couldn't bear. His body, which had been trembling in front of the photograph, collapsed to the floor and balled up fetal again, rocking slightly as if to some distant hymn only he could hear. I had to pick him up, his body startlingly light, as if his bones were made of balsa wood, as if he were some clever disguise of a man filled with a gas lighter than air and not a man at all, and carry him back to the couch where he curled himself up tighter. His mouth kept opening and closing, but no more sound came out, just little dribbles of ash down his chin, and less of that than there had been the day before. The fire, I imagined, must be running out of fuel inside him. My visitor was, with each day, becoming more of a human being and less of a collection of fuel for what fire raged on inside him. That night, he even managed to eat some of the dinner I prepared for us, though he didn't try again to speak.

The next morning I found him seated at the table, hunched over, his arms indicating motion. He was writing. He had found some paper left by my grandfather, no doubt, somewhere in the cabin, and a pencil, and he was frantically writing. When he became aware of me in the room with him, he picked up several sheets of paper filled with the crimped scribbles of words and handed them to me. He wanted me to read what he had written, this was clear in the way he handed the papers to me and nodded to them before going back to work on the page not yet filled on top of the pile of papers still in front of him. I went over to the couch and sat down to read what my visitor had written.

You cannot begin to know what your care for me has already meant, he'd scrawled. Think of this as gratitude, though the story I'm about to tell, you may not find easy to believe. Had I not lived it, I might not believe it. But you have seen the results. You have cleaned my body and tended my wounds and seen the ash that drifts in my breath. Still, you are no Thomas and I am no savior, and doubt is more the fashion now. In that old story, the doubter's seen as a fool who cannot believe that which he feels must be true. The calling for evidence is a failure of faith, the lesson the need to hold to faith without evidence. That is, in fact, the story tells us, exactly when faith is needed, when no evidence is possible. You should not need proof, the story tells us. Today, to believe without evidence is considered the province of the weak-minded, those who do not know enough, or how, to question. To doubt, to know how to doubt, is lauded. So, you must decide if the evidence of my flesh is proof enough. All I can do is tell my story and offer my flesh as the living proof of what I say.

My visitor was a religious man. The way he wrote of the story of Thomas it was almost impossible not to think of him as a holy man, a preacher perhaps. Think of it, an acrobat-preacher. A man of God who flings his wingless body through the smoky air of a carnival, shouting out scripture to the grounded and lost beneath him. Remember, my visitor was still sitting at the kitchen table, naked, writing his smoked heart out. It was easy to look over at him and imagine him flitting through the dust-shrouded air under the tent of some broken-down travelling circus. Easy to picture that lean, sculpted body, covered but not covered by the thin sheen of some reflective fabric stretched so taut over his muscled flesh as to seem just another flesh, dancing solitary in the air to the rhythms of some familiar gospel tune or hymn, finishing his performance by making of his own flesh and bone a crucifix in the hallowed air under the circus' tent.

Almost a month ago, the burned acrobat had scribbled in his taut scrawl, was when it started. Back then, I worked most days pulling crates out of the box cars of trains. The pay was decent and the hours flexible, in that my cousin owned the warehouse where the crates were placed. He'd call me and let me know when a shipment was due in, and pay me more than he should have for my labor.

I told myself this was what my visitor did in the off-season, when the circus stopped travelling and he only preached on Sundays, grounded like the rest of us, in some church whose rafters he only flew through in his dreams.

I had just finished five hours of lifting crates, the acrobat-preacher went on, and was ready to head for Billy's, this bar just down the road from the warehouse. It was dusk, which as you know is a time when animals, like deer and such, tend to be more active. Things seem to come out more at dusk, is the way I've always heard it said.

Anyway, it was dusk, and there I was, like some nocturnal animal, coming out the warehouse, all sweaty, covered with soot. The neon sign swirled Billy's into the darkening air, its glow not so bright as it'd be in a few hours. Black and bickering birds were filling up the trees, lost in the green shadows of the leaves, their chattering and the occasional feather drifting down making the birds themselves easy to assume. Had I known what was about to begin, I might have turned the other way after I'd left the warehouse and gone directly home, collapsed onto my bed and stayed there till it was safe to come out again. But not one of us has ever known what was coming, except Jesus.

The almost flickering light of Billy's colored the humid air, the big B forming vague sideways arches in the moist air that reached well beyond the confines of the glass that held in the neon burning itself into a strange kind of earthly glory. That was where I was headed, the faint ghosts of lettered light semaphores guiding me in.

This part of my visitor's story was hardly mysterious. I had seen this sign the same way many nights, nights I stayed in town to drink. As you, friend, must have seen the sign over this place many times, guiding you in to stories and drink.

Seven beers later, he'd scrawled, I struggled past the bodies of men I only knew the first names of and burst out into what turned out to be thick fog. Dusk was a memory. It was fully night, and the fog, reflecting the light from Billy's and the street lamps, those not burned out or busted by beer bottles hurled drunk, seemed to be a thick, drifting light itself, twisting up around itself as if to wring some guilt out. It took a minute to convince my numb body to head out into that coiling light, and when I stumbled off into it, west, toward home, that was when I noticed the smoky light was roiling more urgent in a patch directly ahead of me, in the path I had to follow home, like it was being stirred, like everything, this light and this fog and whatever world it drifted through, all of it, was in some black kettle on some stove somewhere, and whoever had poured all this together was trying to stir it so all the flavors blended just so. Who would cook this up? was what I thought in the blur of the beers.

The stirring didn't last long, though. She came out of that patch of agitated fog and light which drifted off around her only to gather again behind. Who had conjured her, I couldn't say. Was it the light or the fog, the night or the alcohol, or my battered and bitter heart, I wondered, that had conjured her up out of the smoke?

This was the last of what my visitor had scratched out on the pages he'd given me. While I had read them, the acrobat-preacher had made his way, silent, back to the couch and was asleep under the thin blanket, whatever he had written while I read still clutched in his hand. Though he seemed exhausted, I didn't notice any ash, either at the table where he'd been writing or on the blanket under his breath. Whatever fire it was that had been burning in him seemed to have been put out finally by his beginning to write out his story. Strange, what it is that heals us sometimes, isn't it, friend?

That night, before I went to bed, I heard something I'd only heard once since my visitor had arrived: someone else's voice. It was not a man's voice but the sweet voice of a woman, singing a hymn I seemed to remember hearing my mother sing while she swept out the kitchen or washed dishes. Though she'd stopped praying before I was born, the hymns she learned as a girl still came out now and again, as if they came out of her only when she wasn't guarding what she let go of. It was one of those hymns, something about the grace of God entering the world as a flame, burning everything into a new and brilliant form. It was a woman's voice, without question, but not my mother's voice, with her bitterness making that music darker than it was ever meant to be, more threatening. No, this was a voice full of a sweetness I had never known, a voice so graceful and light it didn't seem it could come out of a human throat. This was the sort of voice, I was sure, that would come from the throat of some heavenly creature. An angel's throat was the vessel such a voice must come from, I thought.

But that voice was coming from the charred and smoky throat of my visitor. I stood over his sleeping figure in the dark until I was sure. I leaned over him, my own sad body swaying with the sweet lilt of that beautiful, inhuman voice rising out of that ruined throat, a throat that only ash and one feeble, febrile name, Phineas, had crawled out of. A throat that had been leaving behind tracks of ash I had to wipe up. That such a voice would come up out of such a throat seemed an affront to the voice and to the world the throat smoked in, a broken ruin. I wanted to feel the affront, like it was something personal, something more than just a miracle involving the physical body, still pretty much in ruin, of my visitor, this acrobat-preacher, this broken man whose lean body was made for flight.

That sweet voice from his dark throat was meant for me, of that I was sure. Who else was there to hear it but me? My visitor himself, for whom any articulate sound was a clear struggle, was sound asleep. And we were alone in the cabin. Either that voice, and its music, was meant for me, I knew, or no one. And that I refused, and still refuse, to believe. Had you heard that woman's voice, you, too, friend, would refuse to believe she sang for no reason.

When the woman who was not there stopped singing through my visitor's charred throat, I went to bed and slept, and dreamed of preachers, draped in albs that burned a white too hot to look at directly, floating through the charred rafters of a ruin of a cathedral. Their lean, muscled bodies, hidden under the blinding robes that left them almost without form in the stagnant air of that shell of a church, were a kind of music in that air, a music I heard, a music from no throat, whole or in smoldering ruins. That music, which seemed to be the very air in the dream, that not only was a part of the acrobats' bodies but also what held them aloft in their luminescent robes, that music was the sweet voice of a woman humming a tune not one of the preachers of the air could hear without weeping, and they were, all of them, weeping, as they flung themselves from rafter to rafter all night in my sleep.

The next morning, after my visitor and I had breakfast, I gathered up the dishes to clean them and he went back to scribbling his story with a pencil sharpened with a steak knife. After I finished with the dishes, he handed me, with the same nod, another sheaf of papers he had filled the day before and that morning, before going back to the scratching down of his tale.

Whoever or whatever had conjured her up out of that fog, I could tell she needed help, he had written. She was in bad shape, that much was obvious, not so much walking as lurching from one stumble through to the next, each time she didn't just collapse into the thicker ground fog a miracle of sorts. The dress she wore had the look of having been pulled on in a hurry, it didn't seem to hang exactly right from her shoulders and seemed caught, somehow, around her lower rib cage, like it was snagged on something there. When she exhaled, the fog did remarkable dances around her face, waltzes they could have been, all that regal dipping and swirling that must have been in time to some music I certainly had never heard before.

She wasn't old but looked worn. The bruise, black on her cheekbone, faded to grey and purple around her eye, and the bruise on one edge of her mouth seemed to pull her face off center. Her lower lip was, or had been, bleeding, and there was a gash across her left cheek all the way to her neck. Despite whatever war she'd been through, despite the fog and the late hour, her eyes startled and shamed everything with the savageness and grace of their color. To call those eyes blue was to deny even the sky the color blue.

Whatever she held in her left hand reflected light from one of the streetlamps, I suppose, though through that fog how any light could be picked up and then intensified in reflection is something I cannot explain. Her arms were crisscrossed with what must have been dozens of gashes, blood still trickling out to seep down over her hands and drip into the fog. Several of the gashes, on both arms, crossed just above the wrists, and it was then I knew at least part of what was happening. What glittered in her hand was a shard of glass, what must have once been part of some bottle. She looked up and saw me just a couple of lurches away and collapsed down into the ground fog, almost invisible, almost as if I had imagined her appearance, or as if she were some ghost who had found, once again, the spot where she had been, when alive, murdered, the spot she was now doomed to stumble her way to every night, only to collapse into it to wait for the next night and the next struggle to fall back into that death, again and again.

But she was no ghost, that I knew for sure when I kneeled down and touched her damp hair. She was so light in my arms I imagined she was not a woman after all, but an angel caught in some kind of evil storm and forced to the earth to lurch through the fog in search of some way back to whatever heaven it was she'd been pulled out of.

I carried her home to my apartment over the hair salon and tended her wounds while she slept. After cleaning the gashes along her arms as best I could, I ripped a couple of old shirts for bandages, pulling the cloth tight over the criss-crossed gashes near her wrists. By the time I was done with her arms and starting to clean out the cuts on her cheek and lower lip, I was falling in love with the fragile creature who had fallen so far to come to this.

How bad our sight is, sometimes, my friend. Bad enough we can look at what is right before us and not see it, but only what we wish it to be.

The whistling of the tea kettle must have been what woke her, that almost human, but thin, screaming. I heard the rustle of cloth and turned to find her huddled against the headboard of the bed, knees at her chest, her wounded arms wrapped tight around her legs, so tight I feared for the bandages, for the wounds below them. More bleeding was not something she needed. Much more bleeding and her skin would pale enough she might actually disappear there on my bed. Her mouth was open and, if she had had the strength, no doubt the scream of the tea kettle would not have been the only scream in my apartment. Given the thin walls in that place, it was a blessing she couldn't make any sound. Had she screamed, more than one of my neighbors would have dialed 911 and the police would have come knocking and no doubt taken her away from me then and there.

Please, I said to her, don't be afraid. I carried you here and tried to clean you up a little. I won't hurt you, I promised her. But she stayed like that, her arms wound tight around her legs until she lost consciousness again and sagged a little, still in the same defensive position.

It was days she spent on that bed, in that position, at least the time I was awake. What she did when I would fall asleep, finally, on the couch, I can't say, but each time I jerked back into being aware of where I was, she was there, on the bed, in the same position, only looser or tighter. I began to fear her limbs had locked in that position, and she would never be able to straighten out again, that I would have to carry her wrapped up like that everywhere, that she would never speak to me, just open then close her mouth when I asked her what she wanted or how she felt. Twice I turned down offers from my cousin for work, afraid to leave her alone in her condition.

One day I woke up and the bed was empty. She was in the chair which faced the couch, still in her wrapped position, but looser than I'd seen it since she took it up, and something else was different, too. It took me a moment to realize what it was, to recognize I'd been hearing something without being quite aware of hearing it. She was humming a tune that sounded like a hymn. By that I don't mean I recognized the tune as a particular hymn, I mean it sounded the way a hymn would sound. She wanted to talk to me, that was the feeling I got, but wasn't quite ready yet. So she sat all curled up in that chair and hummed, her eyes following me from the couch to the kitchen and back. She refused my offer of food that morning, though she was shaking her head less and less viciously when she refused. I guessed she was getting used to me being there, or that I'd been there long enough without hurting her that she was beginning to believe I did not want or mean to hurt her. Someone had hurt her and hurt her bad. Just how bad I would soon learn.

Since this was where the text I had been given that day ended, I had to wait to discover what my visitor, who was asleep on the couch again, the thin blanket over him, papers clutched in his hands under the blanket, had learned about the damage done to *his* visitor.

Such a strange succession of visitations. My visitor had been visited himself, by a figure who haunted him still. What had this woman to do with the fire that had left my visitor speechless? That night there were no preachers hurling themselves among the rafters of a ruined cathedral. My sleep that second night of my visitor's scribbled story was inhabited, instead, by the lurching figures of naked women, women with such grotesque damages done to them they could not be said to be more than troubled ghosts of living women. Legs were twisted and bent back until one foot dragged upside down while the other bore all the weight it could. Some were missing the lower half of a leg altogether, loose flaps of skin making obscene noises against the ashen bones of knees. Some stumbled on the bloody stumps of ankles, feet gnawed off by some vicious hound or rodent. Through it all, as if from some far-off church, came the faint sounds of an organ playing the opening of the hymn my visitor had sung in his sleep in some woman's voice, and then the unmistakable sounds of a choir, a whole choir of women, singing the words of the hymn, though from the distance they were not words, just the sounds of human voices in music. There were other damaged limbs, too. Arms whose hands had been bent back and stapled, open and almost pleading, to the forearm, or broken in the other direction, so the hand grasped the arm it bent at the end of. I saw hordes of these maimed women, all of them, no matter how horrid their damage, naked and moving as best they could, almost as if they were a parade, as if this was some kind of celebration, as if they expected to be cheered by crowds lining some street of the damned. They lurched and staggered and stumbled through my dreams, waving their twisted and broken appendages as if at a crowd. Then there *was* a crowd, and it was a parade, the sounds coming from the mouths of what appeared to be a cheering crowd raspy screams and moans, mixed with the sounds of all those limbs being broken. From out of the mouths of that crowd came torrents of ash that settled on the broken, naked women like some kind of forgiveness, like some kind of love.

After a night of such dreams, I wasn't sure about reading further the scribbles of this poor, haunted acrobat-preacher who had passed through whatever fire he had passed through to find himself at my door. My visitor was at the table, scribbling away, and as soon as he saw me he stopped long enough to hand me another sheaf of papers. I poured myself a cup of the coffee my visitor had made and sat down, not without some fear, to learn just what damage *his* visitor had endured before collapsing in front of him the night of the fog that had been thick enough to hide almost any sin.

The following day, the preacher of the high-wire wrote, her bruises beginning to sink back under her skin and the bleeding all but stopped, which I only knew from changing her bandages the night before while she slept, she woke before me and had fixed a breakfast for the two of us, eggs and hot cakes and bacon and coffee, and was sitting at the table, almost smiling, waiting for me. Her smile didn't seem to fit quite right on her face, what with all the swelling not having gone down. Still, the effort was encouraging, as was the food itself. As we ate together, she told me her story.

It was my own fault, after a fashion, she started. *Since I was little, I had pestered my mother for word of my father. For years, all she would say was my father was a man of God, was off doing God's work and that I was part of his doing of God's work in the world. I was special, my mother always said. I'd been born from a union of love pure as could be, as close to God's own love for the world as human love gets. But I needed to know my father, to put my arms around his body and smell his scent around me and feel his breath in my ear as he whispered my name with the tenderness only a father can feel for his daughter.*

As I got older, I badgered my mother and everyone else in town for more information about my father. In bits and pieces, I came to know more about him, about his particular brand of holiness. I learned he was a healer, that's what they called him. They said he'd travelled with a number of preachers over the years, providing spiritual healing to go along with the preaching of God's word. They said he was a very brave and strong man, that God had chosen him and given him a power, that's what they said it was, a power from God. Finally, I learned about his night wounded in the swamp and his swallowing of worms.

But it wasn't till I was all but grown up that I learned, from my mother as she lay dying in her bed, that my father, Phineas she said his name was, was still alive. He wasn't swallowing worms no more, wasn't doing God's work in the world no more either, far as she knew. Mostly what he's swallowing these days, *my mother told me in her raspy, whisper of a voice,* is whiskey, *and, she said, she'd heard he'd knifed a man in a bar fight and spent some time in county lock up for his crime. It wasn't till she was almost completely gone my mother mouthed the name of the town where she'd heard he was last. I guess, though she didn't want me to know him, she was more fearful of leaving me alone in the world. Maybe she thought the arrival of a daughter would redeem him. Whatever she thought, and despite all my badgering of her over the years, it would have been better for her to leave me alone in the world than to send me to him, though of course there was no way she could have known, dying in her bed like she was.*

After her funeral, I got on a bus and headed for the town whose name my mother had whispered to me her last night on this earth. Didn't know what I'd say to him if I found him in that town. I figured something would come to me when my father was standing in front of me, whatever he smelled of.

I found him just where my mother feared I would, drinking in a bar, the very one you were coming out of when I collapsed in front of you. I suppose, had I grown up with drinkers around me, I'd have been more careful, but my mother didn't date much as I was growing up, and would never date a man twice who drank.

When I came up to my father in that bar and told him who I was and he put his arms around me and pulled me to him, I believed he accepted me as his daughter. He proclaimed me as such to his friends, all drunk around him in the bar, and they all cheered and hugged me and bought him more drinks. And bought me drinks. It was a celebration, though not the kind I had envisioned growing up dreaming about meeting my father. Still, it seemed my father was celebrating my arrival.

When he got me home to his shabby little house near the edge of town, though it could better be said after I got us there, as I had to keep him upright, and had to pick him up off the cement more than once, I learned what was really in his heart, and it had nothing to do with accepting me as his daughter. As soon as we were inside he stood up from leaning on me and put his arms around me and started whispering in my ear. But it wasn't my name he was whispering, but things he was going to do to me. I tried to pull away and discovered that, for all his being drunk, his arms were more than I could overcome. And when I called him Father, that's when his anger came out.

He let me go long enough to slap me hard across my face, and when I whimpered, Father, please, *he struck me again, this time with his fist, before pulling me against him again. He held me pressed against his body with one arm and with the other he tore my dress from my shoulders and pulled it down my body till it was wrapped around my legs. His free hand pulled at the back of my bra till the snaps broke and he ripped it off over my head, pulling some of my hair, caught in the busted snaps, with it. It was then he forced me to my knees in front of him and started grinding his pants into my face. He pulled me back long enough to unzip. His hands were around my neck and squeezing, and he was breathing hard and talking.*

Swallow this worm, sister, *he said to me, his voice almost not human.* Swallow this here worm, the last of its kind. Swallow it and be saved. *As he said this he tried to push himself into my mouth. When I bit down he screamed and jerked back and took one hand off my neck and made it into a fist and hit me, hard, right on my mouth. But that was only the first punch. He kept hitting me until I was cowering on the floor, rolled up in a fetal position, trying feebly to protect myself from his drunken pounding.*

He was cursing God and women as he pounded on me. He pulled me out of the ball I was in so he could rip my underwear off and hit me down there, too. I'll teach you, you little whore of Babylon, *he shouted at me, and placed his fist down there and pushed and pushed until he had shoved it up inside me. That was when I blacked out, with his fist inside me and his words turning more and more inhuman, a growl in the blackness.*

When I came to, I was naked on the floor, and could hear him snoring beside me. From the light coming in through the one window in the room, it must have been the moon or some nearby street lamp, I saw him lying there, his limp member in his hand. His semen was seeping out of me. I pulled myself to my feet. It was a tiny, one room shack he lived in, and it was filthy. There were cockroaches crawling over his legs and I slapped at my own body to make sure none were on me. The stench was horrid, a combination of rotting fruit and meat and burned cigarettes mixing with something else, something that must have been his own odor.

In that vagrant light I got dressed as best I could. My undergarments were useless, ripped as they were. Even my dress had been stretched out and didn't hang right over my body. His snoring kept up. He was dead to the world, is what I thought standing over him in that stinking place, and then I thought he should be dead to the world. He should be dead. I thought no one could fault me for killing him as he slept there on the floor, his disgusting self-proclaimed worm in his hand. So I grabbed an empty beer bottle from the pile in the corner and broke it on the edge of the kitchen table. I would use that sharp sliver of glass to cut off his member and leave him there, his hand empty, to bleed to death. I stood over my father with that sharp dagger of glass in my hand, and couldn't bring myself to do it. I could not bring myself to kill my father.

I decided, instead, I would have to kill myself. If I could not kill him for what he had done to me, I would kill myself for what had been done to me. Either way, any memory of what had happened to me would be ripped from the world. I doubted he would remember what he had done when he woke from his stupor, and so, with me gone, it would be like what he had done to me never happened. I started to tear at my arms and wrists with that shattered glass, stumbling out into the fog as I cut at myself, not wanting him to wake to find my body in his shack, afraid of what he might do to my corpse should it be there when he woke. I stumbled through the pain and the fog, slicing at my arms, until I collapsed. That must be when you found me and brought me here and cared for me, she said, and tried again to smile.

Though it was day outside, she was exhausted. I suggested she get some sleep, and tomorrow I'd take her some place she could get some clothes, and then we'd see about dealing with that wreck of a man she called a father, that devil whose name, she told me, was Phineas. I thought I could help mend her, I really did. I believed that with tenderness and time I could start to heal the wounds inside her, the wounds to her spirit, the way I had started to mend the wounds left in her flesh by her father's attack. Hell, my friend, I actually believed she could be healed, that I could heal her, that I could heal everything. The next morning, she was gone.

My visitor was once more asleep on the couch, naked under the thin blanket, when I finished reading. Time seemed to be holding to no particular order. Hell, I didn't even know for sure, friend, whether it was night or day outside, or just when it was my visitor had arrived. It was hard to remember he had come to my door alone, no woman, bruised or not, with him. The woman, his visitor, haunted the space we shared. A woman's voice was humming the hymn I had heard before, coming from the wrecked throat of the acrobat-preacher as he slept on the couch after wearing himself out writing his story, this story of a visitation by a tortured and tormented woman he pulled up out of the fog and carried home to tend to.

Lying in my bed, I listened to that ghost of a voice humming a hymn about resurrection and glory, and when I dreamed I dreamed of the night my visitor had heard the story of this woman who now, somewhere outside my dream, was humming, through the wrecked throat of the man who had tended to her wounds, some music that needed faith to go with it, to complete it. My visitor was asleep, but the woman, the woman who still hummed out of his throat, was not sleeping.

She was pulling at the ripped strap of her dress and tying it so the dress would not slip off her shoulders. She slipped her unbruised feet into her shoes and stood over her benefactor, this man who had tended to her wounds and ended up charred and broken at my door. In my dream, the woman bent over to kiss him on his forehead, gently so as not to wake him, and, leaving what little money she had in her purse under a glass on his table, the only kind of payment she could leave for him, she left his apartment, closing the door with almost no sound. Outside, it was fog again, but then this was a dream, after all. Isn't there always fog, at night, in dreams, especially dreams of abandonment?

Surrounded by fog in this, my dream of the woman my visitor had given me to be haunted by, she moved slowly, still holding her ribs where the bruises were not yet hidden under the flesh. At first there was only fog and the battered woman walking through it. Then there were the sounds of a river, the slapping of water along the shore and the circling sounds of river birds crying out to one another through the fog and the dark. The woman moved toward the sounds of the river in the dream, her dress, despite her efforts, beginning to slip from her left shoulder. Pulling it up over and over was a pain that made her grimace, heading for the water.

As the river sounds grew louder, a shape began to assert itself in the fog, the lanky shape of a bridge it was, a bridge over the river, and the woman was on the bridge, which swayed slightly under her trembling legs, looking over the railing down to the river. The fog was too thick for her to see all the way down to where the water surged past under the bridge, heading, she thought, toward the gulf and then the ocean, a body of water large enough, she believed, to dilute even her grief and pain to where she could drink it down and not be poisoned by it as she was at that moment, standing there on that bridge.

Poisoned too, by guilt. Guilt that it was she who had tracked her father down, she who had put her arms around him in that bar and kissed his rough cheek, she who had drank with him and all those strangers until she gave in and danced for them after they lifted her onto the table her father had cleared off with a swipe of his huge arm. Guilt that she had let him lean on her all the way to the shack where he slept off his nightly binges. Guilt that she hadn't been strong enough to fight off her drunken father, that she hadn't been strong enough to cut off his member while he slept so he would be left holding nothing while he bled to death on that filthy floor.

Only an ocean, she knew, held enough water to clean that floor or to water down her pain and grief and guilt.

And then, in the way of dreams, she was no longer standing on that slip of a bridge. The fog surrounded her as her body fell through it, fell toward a river she still could not see, a river that would carry her, breathless and bloating, toward the ocean she believed was her only hope of cleansing, of finding her way, still, to heaven, of cleaning the ghost of her father off and out of her body. Her body finally hit the water and the sound was more than the sound of water sidetracked on its way to some gulf and then an ocean, more than the sound of water smacked with flesh, it was also the snapping of small bones up and down her back, vertabrae coming loose and dancing as if to the music of the river's surge under her reddening skin.

Her body, drifting with the current, soulless, wasn't alone in this water which was suddenly cold, which carried her body but did not cleanse it. This river was full of worms, worms the like of which I have only seen in a photograph of a man I'd been told was some sort of relation to me, a photograph my visitor had pointed to and whispered his only articulate sound. *Phineas*, he had rasped at the picture, as if the word were an accusation, which, of course, it was, Phineas being the name of this floating corpse's father, the father who had raped her and sent her into the fog off that bridge, into this river where she floated, breathless, toward the feeble hope of salvation in some ocean somewhere.

This Phineas, this swallower of worms who was related somehow to me, according to my grandfather and my mother whose promise to tell me how was left unfulfilled, this demon of a man had, in the dream, infested the water with his worms, and they swam toward her body and seemed to be kissing the wounds and the bruises, as if they meant to heal what she had been through. The sounds at first were the familiar sounds of lips on flesh. But it didn't take long for the sounds to change, for it to become clear the worms were not kissing her flesh but nibbling at it. The worms had come to feed on the body of the woman floating down the river. The worms were feeding, first, where her flesh was cut or bruised or reddened, but it wasn't long before the worms were devouring the whole of her body. By the time she reached the gulf, bones would be all that were left, bones, loosed by the devouring of every single tendon that once joined them together in the singular form of a woman, drifting apart from one another and sinking towards the filth at the bottom of this river. Bones falling through water was the last image the dream gave me before I woke to what was late afternoon light streaming in across the bed.

Half the day was gone, and so too, it seemed, was my visitor. A search of each room turned up some missing clothes and no trace of the acrobat-preacher, except for a sheaf of scribbled-on papers left on the kitchen table, weighted down with an empty glass. This was the last of his story, and, I feared, the last I would hear from him.

After I found her gone, he had written, I thought I'd just let it go at that, forget what she had told me. That night, I thought, I'd head out to Billy's and drink until memory choked and, its feeble arms slapping at the water, went under. Memory, I wanted to believe, had lungs but no gills, enough drink always fatal, memory's limbs too frail to keep itself from going under. I did wonder where she had gone, but steered away from that, afraid I would end up having to curse myself for not going out after her, afraid of what she might end up doing out there alone in the world, that she might finish off what she had started the night I found her and carried her home and cared for her. Guilt, it turns out, is an amphibious little cuss, its limbs as strong in the water as on land. No amount of drinking will ever drown guilt.

I spent the day removing every trace of her from my apartment. That should make it easier, was what I was thinking, to forget about her, and if I could forget she had ever been there, then maybe the guilt, that clung to her memory the way remora cling to the devouring bodies of sharks, maybe that guilt would, without the memory of her body to feed off, die and sink to the muck at the bottom of whatever body of water all this was swimming around in. The algae-filled pond, with one of those fountains found in ponds in parks in the Midwest, that I imagined my heart was.

That night, in Billy's, half-drunk before ten, I learned more about the nature of that murky pond than I ever cared to. Starting in on my fourth draft, following my second shot of Beam, I heard someone say the name Phineas.

There he was, not ten yards away from me, leaning on the bar talking to the bartender who was pulling him a beer and nodding. The bartender, this grizzled old geezer, started giggling and then it was a full-throated laugh as he handed Phineas the beer. Again, the name was shouted from one of the tables in the back, blurred by the thick smoke in the bar. I couldn't make out who it was calling, but I watched the creature turn towards where the shout of his name had come from and raise his fresh glass of beer in salute to whoever it was back there, whoever it was who thought this beast should be spoken to.

The fact he was out drinking and slapping the backs of men he probably would have insisted were his friends, though none of them knew his full name, that he could be so sociable just days after what he had done to his own flesh and blood, was more than I could stomach. I had seen her body, what he had done to it, the bruises and blood he had left on her in his wake. Hell, my friend, she'd been right to think he probably would not remember what he'd done to her. Either he didn't remember, which in itself was bad enough, that he could do such a thing to his own daughter and have no memory of it just days later, or he was so completely evil that he did remember and could still be out drinking and laughing. I even imagined what had made the bartender laugh was something Phineas had said about the woman he'd been with a couple of nights ago. My god, was he that depraved, that completely evil, that he could actually be bragging about what he'd done to his own daughter?

I kept him in sight from the bar where I kept drinking, but made sure I was sober enough to do what I knew I had to do. When he left it was almost closing, and I was close to sober, having been drinking Cokes for the last hour or so. With every roar of his despicable laugh, I had hardened myself to the task I knew was mine. His daughter might already be dead somewhere, having leapt from some bridge or cut herself enough to finally bleed to death, her corpse might be feeding fish or crows and coyotes, but I, who had tried to heal the damage this bastard had done to her, I would make sure he did not live to keep bragging of what he had done. I followed him through the quiet streets, keeping my distance. When he went into a filthy little shack set back a ways from the road, near some abandoned rails, I waited a few moments before going up and knocking on the door.

When he opened the door with a slurred, inarticulate sound, I kicked it wide open and him onto the floor where just nights ago he had beaten and kicked his daughter before raping her. I stepped in and closed the door behind me and the stench of the place almost knocked me over. *Where did you do it?* I shouted at his whimpering old body crawling across that floor. *Was it here?* I shouted, my hand over my nose, and kicked him in his side. He collapsed into a fetal position, and I kicked him again. *Is that her blood, you bastard?* I shouted as I kept kicking him. *Your own daughter*, I shouted. *How could you do that to your own daughter, you sick fuck? She came to you to find a father, and look what you did to her.* I had never heard my voice like this before, like it was the voice of some frenzied preacher who believed he was in a battle with the devil himself.

Kicking him seemed to calm me some, and that calming slowed me down enough to notice his shirt, which was already damp with his own blood, had bunched up around his ribs, exposing one side and part of his pale, filthy back. It was then I saw the tattoo.

Since I was a child, my mother had told me the story of my absent father. My father, she had said, was a holy man, a man who did the work of the Lord, travelling from town to town and helping to bring people to God and through God to actual healing. I always believed my mother just didn't want to admit the name of the local scum who had fathered me and left her to raise me alone, that the story of a travelling holy man was just a way to make me believe my father loved me but loved the Lord more, that he wasn't with us because the Lord had called him to keep moving from town to town doing His work.

All this came back to me as I stood over the whimpering form of Phineas in that filthy room and stared at the tattoo. This tattoo I had heard about before. From my mother. She had told me little about my father other than that he was a holy man, but one of the things she had told me about was a tattoo he had on his side, in the spot where the lance had pierced Christ's skin as he hung on the cross. In that spot, my mother told me, my father had had someone place a tattoo, a rather grotesque tattoo, to hear her tell of it. The tattoo was a crucifix, but not your usual crucifix. Where the body of Christ should have been, hanging from the cross was the body of an oddly-shaped worm, a worm that in its undulations on that cross had become an obscene rendition of a man. *A worm nailed to the cross in the place of Christ*, my mother said. *That's what your father has on his side.* And that's what I saw on the pale, bruised side of Phineas as he crawled across the floor.

This was more than I could bear. I picked him up and threw his battered body across the room, knocking over the one, dimly burning lamp in the shack. Ignoring the lamp, I picked him up and threw him against another wall and grabbed him before he could crumple to the floor and flung him against another wall. I was shouting the whole time I was hurling his nearly limp body from wall to wall, but only God knows what I was yelling. Only God could have made sense of it, I'm sure. It was beyond the sense of men, that much I know. That this vile creature was my father as well, that it was my sister, or at least my half-sister, he had beaten and raped and sent off self-destructive into the night, that such a creature could have managed to inspire love in even one woman, much less two, or how many more I wondered in my fever, all this was just too much. I was in some place beyond words.

How many times I hurled that vile form against those walls I could not tell you, but the last time he fell into the flames that had been consuming the shack. The heat I had believed was just my anger had in fact been the shack around us catching fire. Phineas, my father, was on the floor engulfed in flames, his body so weakened by my beating he couldn't manage much of a reaction to the pain of being burned alive. He held up his right hand and pointed to his chest. That was all he managed before his arm, the hand, and his chest, collapsed into the empty spaces the fire had left under his blackened skin.

I stood there in the flames and watched my father becoming ash and at first did not feel the flames scathing my own skin. I breathed in the ash and soot from that fire and it felt good, smelled pure and clean. The stench of that place of sin and grief had been replaced by an almost holy smell of fire. It wasn't until the pile of ash and bones that had been my father had collapsed several times, until that pile no longer resembled anything like a man, that I became aware that I, too, was on fire, that I, too, was becoming ash. By the time I was able to drag myself out of those flames, past the collapsing roof which cut me as it fell, through an opening into the night where one of the walls I had hurled my father against had stood just moments ago, the flames had done enough damage I wasn't sure I was still living. I limped off towards the woods, only half aware of what I was doing.

Imagine my shock when I came to, being tended to, in a place with a photograph of the demon father I had left for ashes in the fire that had almost consumed me. The world is full of mystery, my friend, or should I say, brother?

God bless you, my brother. May all of us seeded by the demon find peace now.

This was the end of the scribbling on the last of the pages. In the end, in what I at first believed to be his illness, my visitor had come to believe he and I were brothers. Phineas, he had named the worm-swallower in the photograph my grand-father had always said was a relative of mine. Standing in front of that photograph, friend, with the last pages my mysterious visitor, that acrobat-preacher, had scribbled his story down on, I saw, as if for the first time, the edge of the crucifix with the worm tattoo on the swallower's side, stark-edged in the brilliance of the light, no doubt a klieg light, that burned his body into a mystic kind of brightness.

Phineas, I said out loud, as if speaking to that man paused with the worm about to be slid into his throat. Saying the name out loud like that, like my burned visitor had done, the only word he had ever uttered in his time with me, made me feel something deep in my chest, something that struggled in there, as if one of his worms had gotten inside me and was struggling to swim back up and out my own throat. It was then, friend,

I knew what relation the man in that photograph was to me. It was then I cursed my mother, for ever laying down in love or lust with such a man. Phineas, I knew, had seeded me in my mother's womb, just like he had seeded so many other women who had swooned when he healed through the swallowing down of the worms.

How many other brothers and sisters, all walking wounded in this world, do I have? Though it was only in a dream I saw her death, somehow I know our sister is gone. I have already lost a sister. And my brother, my mysterious visitor who came to me burned into a kind of silence, what has become of him? Is he speaking again? What would he say about the story my mother put me to bed with every night of my childhood, that tale of gators and bloody hips collapsing in her arms on a stage? Would he know to put his arms around me and, through that simple gesture of familial love, forgive my adolescence filled with a violence toward others that knew no reason, that lust and loathing that led me to that cabin in the woods and to thinking to cut my wrists and bleed out into the warm water of the bath? Could my brother see in me the same loathing that had kept him in the fire almost too long? The same loathing that had sent our sister over that bridge into the river to be carried out to the gulf and then the ocean?

Is water enough to forgive us? Is there water enough in this world to heal all who are in need of healing? enough to flood those woods and carry off that cabin I left behind after my brother had found me there and left me there, alone? Is the cursed photograph of Phineas floating, even now, on some black tide?

Have you heard the stories, friend, of a naked man who lives in the treetops? He flings himself from tree limb to tree limb, they say, with a grace rarely witnessed in this world. They say he's as daring as he is graceful, doing stunts in the tree tops, all without a net beneath him, that cause their hearts to somersault in their chests, they say. They say swallowing is difficult while watching him swing and dive among the trees. Some say he shouts scripture down at those who stop to watch him, open-mouthed, necks sore from the craning. Others say they've heard him, at night, crying in the tree tops. They say the sound of his sobbing drifting down to them is enough to make them bawl like babies again and hold on to their lovers more fierce than they have in years. Have you heard the stories?

If you see him, friend, his naked flesh gleaming as he leaps through the tree tops, shout up to him. Tell him his brother loves him. Tell him he is forgiven everything. Tell him to come down out of that hell. Tell him to come home.

ALL THINGS ARE DELIVERED UNTO ME

It's not the cane folks notice first, but my breath. The last few years my lungs have grown afflicted by something akin to clogging, and my breathing is a harsh and troubled thing. Used to be I could breathe with the best of them. I've winded any number of men, back in the day. A man would be under me gasping for breath and I'd keep moving over him, my breath coming easy, as if I hadn't exerted myself at all. He'd be clutching at his chest as if he were having a heart attack and I'd smile and let my loosed and long hair tickle his neck as I trailed it over his face and down to his chest. No man ever died under me, though some swore they'd had near-death experiences. Said they'd seen the light. Said surely my body was a temple and what I could do with it was about as far from sin as they could imagine.

Course, since the cane things have been different. Men don't look at my body, hobbled and starting to bend toward the earth, as anything but the flesh in ruin. Wasting away, is what they think of me. They don't get turned on hearing the harsh rasp of my breath. Some of you have told me, dears, that I should consider this troubled breathing some sort of blessing. You deserve some rest, you've said to me. A woman like you should be glad to finally close things up.

You don't know, my dears, how wrong you are. Being open and moist is my nature. Left alone for too long, the wetness can become a kind of weeping. Yes, my dears, I have wept between my legs. It is sorrow to be closed off from the world.

Sorrow is what that boy healer so long ago gave to me. My memory of the healing is foggy, almost nothing at all. Others have told me how I crawled up the aisle toward the altar while the preacher went on in that voice of his which was like water in the humid air of that church, water running down my throat and heading for the swamp between my legs men loved to get lost in back then. One man, who came to my bed regularly of a Thursday evening when his wife was off playing Bingo at the Catholic church downtown told me, one of them Thursdays, he'd been there, in the congregation, that day.

You was never hotter, he told me, than you were up on that altar with your legs wrapped around the cross our Lord Jesus had hung on as you rubbed yourself, moist, up and down it. I swear, he told me, it took everything I had in me my dear wife would call good to keep from climbing out of that pew where she sat damp only with sweat and running up to that altar and stripping you and taking you there in front of that entire congregation. We'd have shown them what love really looks like, I've no doubt, he said. It would have been a genuine revelation, he told me. He said he'd imagined, had he not held himself back, that everyone would have had to grab someone and the church would have filled with the sounds of damp bodies pressing together and the scents of sweat and the mingling of every precious bodily fluid. Nine months later, he said, there'd have been a series of tiny, screaming revelations all over town, just waiting to be taken to someone's milky breasts and given someone's name, right or wrong.

I giggled and came under him, my dears, when he drew the picture for me of that entire congregation getting busy with one another right there in the church.

All I have to remember that day by, other than this sorrow the boy put in me that has followed me through all these ragged years like a stray dog you feed once and can't get rid of ever after, is a tattered yellow dress that's been in plastic in the back of my closet long as I can remember. From what I can piece together, from what others have told me of the healing and from the few scattered bits of what could either be memory or delusion that have come to me now and then over the years, this shredded out-of-style dress is what I wore when I crawled up that aisle and onto that altar and wrapped my arms and legs tight around that cross and begged the boy to heal me. The stains on it remind me of something else, though, something after the healing.

A few hours after the boy touched me and healed me, so they say, and pulled my sweaty body from the cross and left me cowering behind the altar, I swear to whatever God there may really be I was still in some kind of fevered daze from whatever force had compelled me to climb that altar and rub myself against that cold and sturdy cross. Writhing on my bed atop damp sheets I was, whether in horniness or holiness I can't rightly say, no doubt with the same look on my face as that famous sculpture of St. Teresa, when there was a little knock at my door, almost no knock at all, but it came again, and then again, and I called out to whoever was knocking to For Christ's sake come in already. Next thing I knew the boy was standing over me, stripping down to nothing as he spoke.

Much as I'd like to be able to tell you, my dears, what that boy healer said to me while he got naked and took himself in his left hand while his right was I swear to God pointing to heaven, all I have are bits and pieces. God needs you, I swear the boy said. God is love, he cried. Your body is a holy vessel, he said, and this here is the instrument of the Lord our God. I swear that's what he said as he climbed atop me on the bed and ripped my dress as he tried to pull it up over my head and off. By now I had our Lord's instrument in hand and was stroking it and it was no mean instrument. It got so big in my hand, reminded me of the snakes one of the old healers had used to hold the sins of the folks he healed. Got so big it seemed to speak to me itself, though to be sure I was in a fever at the time and none of this may be close to what really happened that night. Though I'm sure the boy was there and naked and on top of me at some point. The rest of this, though it ain't pure conjecture, surely is to be taken, as any kind of witnessing should be taken, with, as they say, a grain of salt. Maybe quite a few grains.

The instrument of our Lord was tearing at me down there and the boy's smooth hands were grabbing at my butt to pull me to him again and again and, and this more than any of the rest of it I can say I'm sure of, the boy's mouth was sucking at my breasts with a kind of frenzy. It was, I remember thinking even then, like the boy was trying to get milk out of my breasts and, though I'd never been pregnant, and never have been due to being injured down there from the ferocity of more than one lover who lost control over me, that night, while the instrument of our Lord tore me to bleeding and a kind of pain I think of now as a kind of holy suffering, my breasts flowed with a sweet and warm milk the boy suckled out of them and swallowed.

You might say, my dears, it was a miracle, the breasts of a woman who never gave birth giving milk, but it seems to me what happened that night in my bed couldn't be anything holy. Seems to me what that boy did to me, while I was still in the grip of his healing fever, was a sin.

What I think I remember is that, when the boy had finished and was putting his clothes back on, his little boy clothes that had hid that instrument, he knelt beside the bed where I lay writhing and bleeding and oozing out what the instrument, of the Lord or of some demon, had left in me, he knelt there on that plain wood floor and picked up his copy of the holy scripture he had thrown down before grabbing hold of himself and started to read from it. I can't remember all he read, but I remember him looking at me over the gilded pages of his Bible and saying, *Come unto me, all ye that labour and are heavy-laden, and I will give you rest.* Then he stood up, I think, and, this I remember clearly, with his right hand, the one not holding the Bible, he was jerking himself off, stroking faster and faster over my body lying in that damp bed. As he started to come the second time, he shouted out, the Bible still in his other hand and open, some words followed by, Says so in Matthew, chapter eleven. *Take my yoke upon you, and learn of me,* he shouted. What else he said just then is a blur in my memory, made so no doubt by the odor of his seed on my flesh. After he had folded himself, still hard, back into his pants and zipped up, I remember, just before he closed the Bible and left me stewing in both our juices, he said, in the gentlest little boy voice you could ever imagine, *For my yoke,* he said, *is easy, and my burden is light.* I remember wondering, my dears, how much of a burden light could be.

Light burdens us all the same, is what I thought lying in the damp of that bed. It is what light lets us see that burdens some of us more than others. Little did I know, lying there then, the sorts of things I'd be capable of seeing.

It was years before I learned of the gift the boy had planted in me with his awkward and savage lust. It wasn't a thing I came to gradually, but of a sudden. One morning I woke up and asked the man snoring beside me to get dressed and go on home to his wife and everything was as it had been so many other mornings. I was who I'd been when I fell asleep, exhausted, in the man's arms the night before. I was who I had always been, the same through man after man, night after night. After the man left and I'd had some coffee to get me moving, I stood under the shower letting the hot water soothe the muscles of my back and my shoulders, as I had done so many other mornings.

I had not thought of the boy healer since the night I left town the week after one of his gators swallowed him from the waist up. I wasn't there when it happened, but the story was all over town and still going strong the next week when I packed up and stole off in the night. I was determined, I thought at the time, to leave my body's longing for men behind me in the town, but it followed me. I couldn't shake it.

Thinking about a gator lumbering off stage with that little boy's mouth probably still praying in the belly of the beast did, my dears, let me shake off what the boy had done to me. Hell, when I was told the story of the gator swallowing the boy by a man whose hands were playing with my breasts hanging down almost in his face as I moved atop his hips in ways I knew he wouldn't be able to handle for long, I forgave the boy what he'd done to me. Course at that moment I had no inkling of just what all it was the boy had done to me, so I guess it was easier to forgive him. It's always easier to forgive anyone from the midst of a fair to middling orgasm, I've learned.

So after having forgiven the boy years before and getting rid of the man from the night before, with the steam of the shower forming around me as I moaned a little under the ministrations of the hot water on the skin still taut over my aching muscles, it was more of a surprise than it was anything else when I thought of the boy faith healer jerking off over my sore and bruising body while quoting out of Matthew. No sooner had I pictured him, his hand stroking so rapidly it was a blur, than I felt a strange light-headedness and reached for the wall of the shower to keep from falling to my knees under the hot water. My hand on the wall seemed not to belong to my body, but it held me up and, as the hot water pounded down, I knew the boy had given me something, a gift in the midst of that cruel passion, and I knew it had grown inside me until it had become a vision, a way of seeing. And seeing is the way to knowledge, and knowledge, as even the Bible-thumpers know, is power. The kind of power that had overtook me that day in the church when I crawled up to the altar and humped the cross.

I was only in the church that day to be overtaken, my dears, because I was fulfilling a man's fantasy of being blown in the back pew of the church during services. The man was just beginning to lose control and starting to moan, his member trembling in my mouth, when my mouth went dry of a sudden and I pulled away from him. He was begging me to finish, all bent over and twisted in a sort of pain I would have laughed at on any other occasion. Laughter wasn't what I was feeling inside, and what I was feeling wasn't just inside but was all around me, too, making the humid air inside that church into a hum and the hum into a music, a hymn my body was one verse of, all the other bodies the chorus. So much music made of so many bodies brought together by faith and the promise of some sort of healing drove me to the floor and set me to crawling toward the center of the composition, the altar where the music that sanctified me somehow seemed to emanate from that cross and made me think, for some reason, as I crawled up the aisle and onto the altar to take it between my legs, of those You Are Here symbols on maps in malls or amusement parks, signs meant to help you find your way by making it clear, by showing you your position, what direction you must move in. To know one's position is all it may take, is the lie such symbols are in the business of telling.

Position is never, alone, enough, my dears, believe me.

I've known them all, and not one congruence of torsos and limbs has anything to do with understanding anything of this world. And don't even get me started on salvation. That's a thing a body has to find on its own. All I know is, those very few I'd say are surely saved do their good works out of earshot of the cross.

It was years before I thought to take advantage of the power the boy had given me out of his horniness. By then, I was already a bit hobbled but the cane was still some years off, and my breathing was still a melody I'd occasionally hear men humming or whistling as they headed for offices or homes and smiled and waved to me, out for my morning constitutional. By then, I'd started to think what was between me and men was some kind of revenge disguised as rapture. By then, all the music and dancing men and women take up as excuses for touching one another was a language I could read without the need for a translator, each contorted body in the crowds of bodies a letter to add to the message. Fuck us, the bodies would spell out over and over. Lie down with us and give yourself over to the music that plays between your flesh and this place your flesh moves in and through. Lie down with us, the bodies would spell out, and see and feel and know what else is within you, what has slept within you since the boy healer placed himself within you and started to move with you and shivered some of what was inside him into you.

Seeing other bodies as letters was the trigger, it seems, as if abstracting the human body allows for a clarity about it that just isn't possible as long as the body is seen as a place the soul resides and where ecstasy can come for a brief stay. My clarity, the gift the boy left to flower inside me, allowed me to put out a shingle, as they say, and charge a pretty penny for what I could tell a couple. This is not, my dears, a question of faith. Faith is not what the boy had in mind or in hand the night he put himself and then the gift inside me. This is about seeing. This is about knowing, and knowing with a certainty I didn't think flesh was capable of all those nights and days I tried to bury myself in the scents and textures of those other bodies.

Couples come to me to learn how to, and when to, place and move their bodies to assure the nature of the child they produce. They come into my shop and they give me what money I ask of them and they tell me what I tell them I need to know in order to tell them how to have the kind of child they say they want to have. What I ask of them isn't easy. They squirm and look out the large bay windows I make sure to seat them across from that open out on a boulevard where trees skitter with the nervous bodies of magpies and grackles and jays and crows. In watching the trees squirm they believe the world outside has taken on their nervousness and this makes it possible for them to go on and tell me what they need to tell me. They sit in my office, which is just the downstairs bedroom of a three bedroom house bought with the cash from my early prophecies, and they recite the passages of their lovemaking, variants on a familiar theme, each unforgettable in its memory and embarrassing in its being related to me, this strange woman with a cane and a raspy voice who offers coffee and scones in the awkward silences that come fewer and far between as the younger man and woman fidgeting as they speak in the dim room start to think less of where they are and more of the places and times they are telling of, the times and places their bodies have been made sacred by their fumbling together, by their desperate grappling on one to the other, their breath near the end almost the breath of the older woman who listens without taking down a single note. I close my eyes and my lips form a smile, my dears, as I listen to memories of fornication made into awkward language, a language as fumbling as the couple's hands at one another's clothes to release the transfiguring nakedness of the bodies hidden all day under cloth.

It's the smile, I overheard one of my customers telling his wife as they left the shop holding one another, already in the pre-trembling of sex, or the expectation of sex, Da Vinci painted on the face of the Mona Lisa. That's her smile.

Later, one of them will dream, lying in sheets damp from sex, of a villa in Tuscany, or some other part of Italy. There will be a human music coming from within the villa, the music of a woman humming a song she remembers only part of, a song that was always on the radio when she was a little girl, and the woman will hum over and over again the part of the song she remembers until she starts to hum the rest of it she makes up, or maybe she thinks she remembers it but can't say if she remembers it the way it really went or not. Around that villa with the human music contained within it rows and rows of vines will buzz with the busywork of bees and it will seem the buzzing of the bees and the humming of the woman inside the villa will take up the same song, and it will seem the light will shiver through the tiny leaves growing along the vines with the same melody, and the day itself will seem to be music, and the one man out tending the vines will start to dance among the rows of vines, and the music his boots make in the damp ground will sound like the music the bodies of lovers make desperate in the fevered act of love.

Which is the music I tap my cane to each night as I fall asleep in my chair.

And the music I'm tapping out right now, my dears, though were anyone to ask I'd probably be tempted to lie and say it was Amazing Grace I had going in my old, gray head, and you'd smile and maybe even believe that's what you'd been hearing. You'd actually convince yourselves I'd been tapping out Amazing Grace, and one of you would start humming it and maybe even singing a bar or two, whatever you could remember of it. And I would relish the irony, that the music made by the urgent pressing together of the naked flesh of lovers could so readily be mistaken for that hymn, for Amazing Grace. Just now, though, tapping the music out with my cane on this wood floor, I'm not convinced it's irony after all. To say the music bodies compose out of love is an amazing grace doesn't seem ironic at all, my dears.

Is it that hymn I hear going back to before my taking of the cross on that altar, or is memory only falling in line in the sweet revisions we come to if we live long enough for our bodies to go quiet? My dears, what music have you heard in what passion you have known? If only I could convince myself that it's all an amazing grace, and not sin. If only that cross had given itself over to my heat and swollen up and slipped inside and left me something other than what the boy left me. Surely that cross could have left me a kind of love, my dears, that could have sustained me and kept my body from its slow bending towards the earth, a kind of love that would have left my body without any sign of gravity's work.

If that cross had been able to fill me with love, maybe I wouldn't have needed to listen to my clients tell me of the histories of their lovemaking. I tell them I need to know this in order to give them a guarantee on my instructions to them, but I confess now, to you, my dears, this was always no more than a lie. All I really need to know is the sort of child they want, a boy or girl, athletic or intellectual, tender or tough, brunette or blond or redhead, and all the rest, and where they live, of course, and I can tell them everything they need to know. What day of the week and at what time they should do it and in what position. I even tell them what each needs to be thinking of as the sperm is released. This, though, comes to me between sessions, and whatever I'm doing when it comes to me I stop and write it down, and it's whatever I've written the thoughts down on I hand to the woman when she and her husband come for the final session, where I will give them their instructions along with their guarantee and all the papers will be signed.

My listening to their sexual histories is just a tormented and tormenting kind of reminiscence, maybe a kind of penitence, one I've indulged in for the smile my clients have noticed, a smile none of them know, my dears, is gone much too quickly, replaced with a kind of gentle suffering that keeps me company for days, often till the next session with a couple who've come to get their guarantee. Mona Lisa's smile has intrigued folks so long cause somehow Da Vinci was able to trap, somewhere in all those pigments and that linseed oil, the body's only possession, the only thing of value it staggers through this world with. Da Vinci was able to capture the awful dichotomy of the flesh, the ritual dance that joy and sorrow, holding to one another with all they're worth, dance, a dance that makes the flesh what it is. The body, oh my dears, is the shape of the music that keeps joy and sorrow dancing with one another for the length of a body's time in this world.

The sorrow the boy left in me, the sorrow that has grown into this vision I share with the couples who come to me willing to pay for it, I think, only stays with me and gives me this vision because my joy of being in my body was so exercised by loving all the men I loved before and after the boy that it was strong enough and sure of foot enough to let the sorrow grow and still hold the sorrow in that dance. My vision is a vision born of polar extremes, and I am beginning to think it is this very dancing together of joy and sorrow with such passion in my body that bends my body toward the ground, that makes this cane a necessity, that makes each breath I take in so harsh.

Or is it that the sorrow that comes to me, after I've sat with those couples and listened to the arcs of their lovemaking, has become too much? Is it that joy isn't able, any longer, to ever lead sorrow in the dance? Is it that listening can't ever be enough, that always one must at some point stop listening to the love of others and do a little loving of their own? Can the loving I did in the past no longer keep me sustained? Just what would love be like for this body so used to leaning on this cane? These are the thoughts, my dears, that helped to bring me here, to this witnessing. These thoughts, and one of those events that all the joy and all the sorrow in the world can't predict, a result of the utter randomness of existence.

A couple months ago on my way home from the corner store, I had taken the long way back, despite the cane, as it was a nice day out and I had no appointments with couples that afternoon, which meant I would be crossing the interstate on the old cement bridge, the one I hear the city's thinking of replacing, saying it's getting old enough it might not be safe what with all the traffic crossing over it every day, more than it was built for. There was a man standing on the sidewalk in the middle of the bridge holding a sign in such a way as to make it easily seen from the interstate below. The sign read Matthew 11: 27-30, like those signs you see someone holding up in the crowd behind the goal posts on Sundays. Having forgotten what little I may have once known of the scriptures, I had no more idea what those verses in Matthew said than I know what message someone is trying to send from behind those goal posts all over the country.

I could have crossed the road and gone by the sign bearer, but he seemed harmless enough. It wasn't like he was shouting scripture or raving about the evils of the world. He was just holding the sign so the travelers in the cars and trucks passing under the bridge had the chance to read it, so that maybe later that night, after he'd checked in to some dingy or bright motel room still several states from home, a man might take the Bible out of the drawer under the TV, where a pregnant woman stands next to a map of the country showing the path of a major storm front, and turn to Matthew, chapter eleven and, starting with verse twenty-seven, start to read, and wonder why that old preacher on the bridge earlier had wanted him to think about how close a father and a son can be, until he gets to verses twenty-nine and thirty and, tired from several days on the road, all that stuff about yokes and rest and easy burdens the boy had ranted over my damp, naked body would seem like a message meant for him, as if God had used that old preacher to speak to him directly, and he might pick up the phone and pause to remember a number and dial it and when a woman said Hello? he might break down and weep and beg forgiveness and ask to come home and, weeping, she might say Yes, honey, come on home.

Don't we all secretly want to believe we can fix up, a little, the world? How much of that moaning and breathing done when I was young and when men wanted to just about burst out their hearts over or under me was a matter of me trying to fix up the world? More than I would've cared to admit then, I think. Course none of it fixed anything in the world, including me, and God knows I needed to be fixed.

On that old and crumbling bridge, on that place of brokenness, that preacher with the sign out over the interstate put the sign down as I approached and held out his hand, which I took, after setting down my small bag of groceries, with the hand not holding my cane, and he introduced himself to me as Reverend Dave of The Church of Jesus Christ Our Lover and, the two of us each aware of the other's brokenness, we sat down on the bench the makers of the bridge had placed there in its center as a rest stop for the weary traveler, and I pulled out a couple of apples and handed him one and we both bit in and smiled as a little juice coated our hands. The sun felt good on our old bodies sitting on that hard but warm cement bench.

Reverend Dave, I said, the name of your church, it's rather unique. How, I asked, did it come to be so named?

And Reverend Dave started in on the story that began with his Martha taking ill and him taking her to a healing with a boy faith healer he said had healed hundreds already that summer. His description of the boy healer set me to shivering, and Reverend Dave took off his suit coat and put it around me and kept on with the story of the gator he cut open on the stage whose gutted stomach gave up the remains of an organist. He didn't tell me right off about the preacher who wallowed in the roiling mess with what was left of the organist. He likes to hold that back for last, to end with that, he says.

With his coat around my shoulders and the cars and trucks passing under the bridge and heading out for places east or west of where we sat, he told me of the next night, of how the gator took that boy healer from the waist up with one swipe of his razored jaws and ambled away from that tent back to the swamp the boy and his helpers had taken him from.

But it were the organist, that perfect face left attached, he said, to an almost nothing body, that stuck in my heart that day and that haunts me still. The face that preacher, Reverend Dave said, mad with what must of been a kind of longing the world ain't seen the likes of since the days just after we'd been tossed out of Eden, when Adam and Eve were wrecks of bodies rapt with memories of paradise, looked at and, blessed in some odd way by his madness and his longing, saw it whole and complete and as a thing of angelic beauty.

And that, my lovely lady, is what love can do, let us look at this fallen and broken remnant of what the good Lord created whole and perfect, out of his own love, and let us see it without all the breaking and the suffering we've wrapped it in.

My dears, I could not hold myself from interrupting the Reverend one more second. That same boy healer, the one the gator walked off with half of, I was healed by him, but before the gators. Reverend Dave had told me how he and Martha had taken the slice of gator the boy handed them home, and had cooked it up just like he told them to and had eaten of it. He had even told me about what happened that night, though he looked out over the interstate when he spoke of his Martha passing beside him and him being unawares till the morning.

That boy you speak of, Reverend Dave, though he may indeed have done some healing, there was darkness in him too. I seen that darkness the very night he healed me, I said, and told Reverend Dave about what he done after the healing and what it had left in me and what that which was put in me by the boy healer's lust had grown into. I told Reverend Dave of my vision.

Reverend Dave was shaking with the cruelty of the revelation when I stopped to catch a raspy breath.

I remember you, Reverend Dave said. Do you remember the man who led you from behind the cross outside to the picnic table loaded down with ham and turkey and potato salad and the like? I shook my head, all that being left rather blurry in my memory. That was me, Reverend Dave told me. The preacher asked me to help you out to the food. She'll be needing her nourishment now, I reckon, I remember him saying. That was me that helped you up that day. The Lord, he does like to work in mysterious ways, yes sir.

My eyes, they were still shut tight in shame, the shame of recollection, I guess, but I could feel Reverend Dave taking me in. It had been some time since a man had given me that kind of look over, my dears, but there was no denying it.

Guess that gator was God's way of setting things right, he said. He could not have said anything more kind to me at that moment. I think it was right there and then, my dears, I fell in love with Reverend Dave.

We sat there on that cement bench and spoke of how it seemed everyone we knew from that time of faith healers in tents at the edges of towns were either dead or gone missing. We marveled at our having found one another on that bridge some were saying was a thing too broken to be any good anymore. And when I agreed to walk with him back to his church to see where he preached, and he bent down to give me his arm to help me up, there was electricity between that arm and my body I had not ever felt, not even back when I was often pressed naked the length of a man I'd talked to the first time earlier that evening. That electricity did not go numb as Reverend Dave let me lean on his arm as he led me back to this place where he's brought so many of you who were once broken and in need of fixing up.

When I asked about the painting hung in the place where I would expect a cross to be, Reverend Dave reminded me of the crazed preacher rolling around with the ravaged body of the organist in the spilled blood and guts of a sliced-open gator, of that holy moment when he grew still and took her dead but perfect face in his hands and kissed her. He didn't need to say anything more. It was suddenly so clear what he had done.

Though he has, since that first night, told me how he went to several artists famous around town for their technique and asked each to paint the icon for his church, The Church of Jesus Christ Our Lover. How each had produced a painting that, while beautiful and technically just what he had asked for, wasn't the icon he needed for his church. How he went out and bought a board and gessoed it and prayed to the Lord for the strength to do what he had to do. How he closed his eyes and, humming Amazing Grace, started painting. How he didn't open his eyes for over eight hours while he let prayer and the melodies of hymns guide his hand and the brush in it. How when he opened his eyes the icon that hangs now over the altar of this church in the place of the cross was whole and complete and as he remembered it, that sacred kiss.

This is it, my dears, the end of my witnessing. Except to give thanks to the Lord for bringing me and the Reverend Dave together to dance some more that dance of sorrow and joy we are, all of us, dancing, whether we know it or not, every day of our lives. Thank the Lord that, cane or no cane, this breath is enough to say I love you. Praise the Lord that after everything else, there can still, and always, be love.

ACKNOWLEDGMENTS

The following stories were first published by the journals and presses listed below. The author is grateful to the journals and presses for first presenting these stories.

Arroyo Literary Review: "Fishing the Sky without Bait";
Eureka Literary Magazine: "The Music of a Thing";
Green Mountains Review: "Old Time Religion";
Moon City Review: "A Very Old Music";
New England Review: "What Gives Us Voice";
Nimrod International Journal: "The Under the Rivers
    Humming Cross of Rome, Georgia";
The Southern Review: "To Give Ghosts the Finger."

"Hymn of Ash" won the 2007 Elixir Press Fiction Chapbook Competition and was published as a chapbook, *Hymn of Ash*, in 2008 by Elixir Press

I'd like to thank the fiction writers with whom I've shared my work over the years and with whom I've had so many conversations about the art of fiction, and please forgive me if I forget anyone here (blame it on the Mad Cow): Douglas Smith, Mairi Meredith, Tom Noyes, Aimee Pogson, Joshua Shaw, Evan Ringle, Nate Carter, Kristy McCoy, Joanna Howard, Paula J. Lambert, Michael Czyzniejewski, Tina May Hall, Wendell Mayo, Sean Kelly, Tasha Hass, Jeff Fearnside, Eugene Cross, Ann Pancake, Brian Evenson, Aimee Parkison, Abby Frucht, Laura Kasischke, Jaimy Gordon, Alberto Rios, Lee K. Abbott, Dan Chaon, Jill McCorkle, Pamela Painter, Aimee Bender, Amy Hempel, Lydia Davis, Melanie Rae Thon,

Mark Brazaitis, and Tony Doerr. And, of course, I'd like to thank Peter Conners for selecting this collection for the BOA Editions Short Fiction Award.

This book is dedicated to Douglas Smith, who taught me more about the art of writing than anyone else, who was my best friend for thirty-six years, and who died much too young.

ABOUT THE AUTHOR

George Looney is the author of three previous collections of fiction that have won the Leapfrog Press Fiction Award, The Elixir Press Fiction Award, and the Elixir Press Fiction Chapbook Award. He has also published thirteen collections of poetry, including books that won The Bluestem Award, The White Pine Press Poetry Prize, and The Red Mountain Press Poetry Prize. He is Distinguished Professor of Literature and Creative Writing at Penn State Erie, The Behrend College, where he founded the BFA in Creative Writing Program and is editor of *Lake Effect* and translation editor of *Mid-American Review* (where he began the ongoing Translation Chapbook Series in 1983). With Phil Terman, he was co-founder of the original Chautauqua Writers' Festival. He hopes to someday make it back to the Irish town of Kinsale in County Cork.

BOA Editions, Ltd. American Reader Series

COLOPHON

BOA Editions, Ltd., a not-for-profit publisher of poetry and other literary works, fosters readership and appreciation of contemporary literature. By identifying, cultivating, and publishing both new and established poets and selecting authors of unique literary talent, BOA brings high-quality literature to the public.

Support for this effort comes from the sale of its publications, grant funding, and private donations.

†

The publication of this book is made possible, in part, by the special support of the following individuals:

Anonymous
Angela Bonazinga & Catherine Lewis
Colleen Buzzard & Hucky Land
Christopher C. Dahl
James Long Hale
Margaret B. Heminway
Charles Hertrick & Joan Gerrity
Nora A. Jones
Paul LaFerriere & Dorrie Parini, *in honor of Bill Waddell*
Barbara Lovenheim
Joe McEleveny
Nocon & Associates, a private wealth advisory practice of Ameriprise Financial Services LLC
Boo Poulin
John H. Schultz
Meredith & Adam Smith
Sue Stewart, *in memory of Stephen L. Raymond*
William Waddell & Linda Rubel